James Hadley Chase and The Murder Room

>>> This title is part of The Murder Room, our series dedicated to making available out-of-print or hard-to-find titles by classic crime writers.

Crime fiction has always held up a mirror to society. The Victorians were fascinated by sensational murder and the emerging science of detection; now we are obsessed with the forensic detail of violent death. And no other genre has so captivated and enthralled readers.

Vast troves of classic crime writing have for a long time been unavailable to all but the most dedicated frequenters of second-hand bookshops. The advent of digital publishing means that we are now able to bring you the backlists of a huge range of titles by classic and contemporary crime writers, some of which have been out of print for decades.

From the genteel amateur private eyes of the Golden Age and the femmes fatales of pulp fiction, to the morally ambiguous hard-boiled detectives of mid twentieth-century America and their descendants who walk our twenty-first century streets, The Murder Room has it all. **>>>**

The Murder Room
Where Criminal Minds Meet

themurderroom.com

James Hadley Chase (1906–1985)

Born René Brabazon Raymond in London, the son of a British colonel in the Indian Army, James Hadley Chase was educated at King's School in Rochester, Kent, and left home at the age of 18. He initially worked in book sales until, inspired by the rise of gangster culture during the Depression and by reading James M. Cain's *The Postman Always Rings Twice*, he wrote his first novel, *No Orchids for Miss Blandish*. Despite the American setting of many of his novels, Chase (like Peter Cheyney, another hugely successful British noir writer) never lived there, writing with the aid of maps and a slang dictionary. He had phenomenal success with the novel, which continued unabated throughout his entire career, spanning 45 years and nearly 90 novels. His work was published in dozens of languages and over thirty titles were adapted for film. He served in the RAF during World War II, where he also edited the RAF Journal. In 1956 he moved to France with his wife and son; they later moved to Switzerland, where Chase lived until his death in 1985.

By James Hadley Chase
(published in the Murder Room)

No Orchids for Miss Blandish (1939)
Eve (1945)
More Deadly Than the Male (1946)
Mission to Venice (1954)
Mission to Siena (1955)
Not Safe to Be Free (1958)
Shock Treatment (1959)
Come Easy – Go Easy (1960)
What's Better Than Money? (1960)
Just Another Sucker (1961)
I Would Rather Stay Poor (1962)
A Coffin from Hong Kong (1962)
Tell it to the Birds (1963)
One Bright Summer Morning (1963)
The Soft Centre (1964)
You Have Yourself a Deal (1966)
Have This One on Me (1967)
Well Now, My Pretty (1967)
Believed Violent (1968)
An Ear to the Ground (1968)
The Whiff of Money (1969)
The Vulture Is a Patient Bird (1969)
Like a Hole in the Head (1970)

An Ace Up My Sleeve (1971)
Want to Stay Alive? (1971)
Just a Matter of Time (1972)
You're Dead Without Money (1972)
Have a Change of Scene (1973)
Knock, Knock! Who's There? (1973)
Goldfish Have No Hiding Place (1974)
So What Happens to Me? (1974)
The Joker in the Pack (1975)
Believe This, You'll Believe Anything (1975)
Do Me a Favour – Drop Dead (1976)
I Hold the Four Aces (1977)
My Laugh Comes Last (1977)
Consider Yourself Dead (1978)
You Must Be Kidding (1979)
A Can of Worms (1979)
Try This One for Size (1980)
You Can Say That Again (1980)
Hand Me a Fig-Leaf (1981)
Have a Nice Night (1982)
We'll Share a Double Funeral (1982)
Not My Thing (1983)
Hit Them Where It Hurts (1984)

I Would Rather Stay Poor

James Hadley Chase

An Orion book

Copyright © Hervey Raymond 1962

The right of James Hadley Chase to be identified as the author of this work has been asserted in accordance with the Copyright, Designs and Patents Act 1988.

This edition published by
The Orion Publishing Group Ltd
Orion House
5 Upper St Martin's Lane
London WC2H 9EA

An Hachette UK company
A CIP catalogue record for this book is available from the British Library

ISBN 978 1 4719 0347 2

www.orionbooks.co.uk

Part One

CHAPTER ONE

KEN TRAVERS, Pittsville's deputy sheriff, sat in his ageing Packard, chewing gum, his mind clouded with the frustrating prospects of his future.

Tall, lean and dark, Travers had an aggressive jaw, grey intelligent eyes and a burning ambition to gain a position in life that would enable him to marry, raise children and have a decent home of his own.

It was frustrating to know that this ambition could only be achieved when the present sheriff either retired or died. Sheriff Thomson, who Travers not only admired but liked, was nudging seventy-six. Travers felt the old man, no matter how smart he happened to be, no matter how good a sheriff he might be, should have retired long ago and allowed him (Travers) the chance to take over the well-paid job of sheriff of Pittsville. Holding that position and with that income, Travers could have married Iris Loring, a nineteen-year-old beauty he had been courting for the past year and with whom he was very much in love.

Apart from these frustrating thoughts, Travers was also labouring under the grievance of having to spend his Saturday afternoon guarding the Pittsville bank when he should have been spending the time with Iris: a date he had arranged and had had to cancel when the news came to the sheriff's office that Joe Lamb, the manager of the bank, had had a stroke.

Sheriff Thomson, who planned to spray his rose trees, had handed the job of guarding the bank to his deputy.

'Sorry, son,' he said with his genial grin, 'but I've important things to attend to. You watch the bank. You never know. Someone might get ideas and there's Miss Craig waiting for the fellow from head office to take charge. I know Iris and you have a date, but this is an emergency. You'll have plenty of time to meet each other week-ends, so go to it.'

Travers had been sitting in the car since half past ten a.m. The time was now three forty-five and all hopes of seeing Iris had now vanished. As he shifted irritably in the car seat, he spotted a dusty Mercury with San Francisco number plates pass him and then slow down as it passed the bank. It drove on to the municipal parking lot. He watched a tall, heavily-built man get out of the car and come walking back towards the bank.

Travers studied the man, his eyes alert. Obviously an athlete, Travers told himself. He had an easy, long stride, his shoulders were broad and he had that springy step that could cover miles without fatigue. Travers had no time to form a further judgment for the man had started up the path that led to the bank doors. Travers got out of his car and moved forward.

'Hey!' he called, his voice pitched so it would carry. 'Just a minute!'

The big man turned and looked around, pausing. Travers joined him in five long strides.

'The bank's closed,' he said and flipped back his lapel to show his badge. 'You want something?'

Now he was close to this man, he was aware of piercing blue eyes, a lipless mouth, a square brutal jaw, but all this suddenly dissolved into charm when the man smiled: it was a wide, friendly smile that softened the brutal lines and made Travers suddenly wonder why he had disliked this man at first sight.

'I'm Dave Calvin,' the man said. 'I'm the new manager of the bank.'

Travers returned the smile.

'Deputy Sheriff Travers,' he said. 'Will you identify yourself, please?'

Calvin took out his bank pass and offered it.

'Will this do? I see you people take good care of the bank when you have to.'

Travers studied the pass, then returned it.

'The sheriff didn't think Miss Craig should be left alone,' he said, 'so I got stuck with the job. Now you've arrived, I guess I'll clear off.'

The piercing blue eyes ran over him. The wide, friendly smile was very evident.

'How's Mr. Lamb?'

Travers shrugged his shoulders.

'He's pretty bad. The doctor says it's touch and go. We'll know by tomorrow if he's going to get over it or not.'

Calvin made sympathetic noises.

'I'd better meet Miss Craig. She'll be glad to get home.'

'She sure will,' Travers said. He walked up the path with Calvin. 'This has given her a shock. She found him on the floor in his office.'

As the two men reached the bank entrance, the door opened and a girl stood in the doorway. Calvin took her in with one quick, searching glance. She was about twenty-five or -six, above medium height and frail looking. The rimless spectacles she wore gave her a spinsterish look. Although she was plain looking, her complexion was good. Her mouse-coloured hair was neat.

'This is Mr. Calvin,' Travers said. 'I thought I'd stick around until he arrived.'

The girl was looking at Calvin: a painful flush rising to her face. Calvin smiled at her. His wide, friendly confident smile coupled with his staring blue eyes generally made an impact on women. It seemed to be having a devastating impact on Alice Craig.

'I'm sorry to have kept you waiting, Miss Craig,' Calvin said, aware of the impression he was making on the girl, 'but it was short notice and I had quite a way to come.'

'Oh ... that's all right,' she stammered. 'I – I didn't expect ... won't you come in?'

Travers said, 'Well, I guess I'll get along. Glad to have met you, Mr. Calvin. Anything I can do, just ask. I'm over the way at the sheriff's office.'

Calvin shook hands with him, then followed the girl into the bank. Travers walked back to his car.

Calvin shut the door of the bank and looked around. It was very small. There was the usual grill-protected counter. Behind this was a glassed-in office. There was a door near him and another door facing him behind the counter. There was a wooden seat for waiting customers and a table on which stood magazines and a vase of flowers.

Alice Craig watched him. He could see she was making futile efforts to control the deep flush that still stained her face.

'I'm sorry about Mr. Lamb,' Calvin said. 'It must have been a shock for you. I'm sure you want to get home. Suppose you give me the keys and then get off? There's nothing we can do now until Monday.'

She looked startled.

'You don't want to check?'

'Not right now,' Calvin said, smiling. 'I'll do all that on Monday.' He moved past her, not looking at her because her embarrassment began to irritate him. He opened the door leading into the manager's office. It was a nice room with a carpet, an armchair, a handsome-looking desk and a high-backed desk-chair. He went around behind the desk and sat down. Alice came to the door and stood looking helplessly at him.

'Come in and sit down,' he said, waving to the armchair. 'A cigarette?'

'No, thank you. I – I don't smoke.' She came in reluctantly and perched herself on the arm of the chair, looking down at her slim, well-shaped hands.

What a type! Calvin thought. She has as much personality as a potato and she's as sexless as a nun.

'Well, now,' he said, keeping his voice mild and friendly. 'How about the keys?'

'They're in the top drawer on the left,' she said, still not looking at him.

He opened the drawer and took out a set of keys. They were all neatly labelled.

'What keys do you hold?' he asked.

'I – I have a key to the front entrance as you have and I have a key to the vault. There are two locks on the vault. You have one key and I have the other.'

He smiled at her.

'So I can't rob the vault without your permission and you can't without mine. Is that it?'

She gave a nervous little smile, but he could see the joke as such wasn't appreciated.

There was a pause, then he asked, 'Can you give me Mr. Lamb's address?'

'The Bungalow, Connaught Avenue. It's the fourth turning on the right down the main street.'

'Thanks.' He made a note of the address on the scratch pad on the desk. 'How about accommodation in this town? What's the hotel like?'

She hesitated, then she said, 'It's very bad. The best and the most comfortable place is where I'm staying. Mrs. Loring's rooming-house. The food is very good and it isn't expensive.'

Calvin realized he had made a mistake by asking her such a question. He had no wish to live where she did, but now, it was impossible for him to turn down her suggestion.

'Sounds fine. Well, okay, let me have the address.'

'It's on Macklin Drive. The end house. It's about a mile and a half off the Downside highway.'

'I'll find it.' He put the keys in his pocket and stood up. 'I guess I'll call on Mrs. Lamb now, then I'll come on to Macklin Drive.' He looked curiously at her. 'How come you don't live with your parents?'

He saw her flinch.

'I haven't any,' she said. 'They died in a road accident five years ago.'

'That's too bad.' Calvin cursed himself. He seemed to be asking all the wrong questions. He moved to the door. 'You lock up. We'll talk business on Monday. I'm sure we are going to get along fine together.'

It amused him to bring the painful flush to her face. He watched it for a brief moment before walking quickly down the path and along the sidewalk to the car park.

He drove to Connaught Avenue and pulled up outside Joe Lamb's bungalow. It was made of brick and timber, showing signs of wear.

Calvin sat in the car for several minutes, looking at the bungalow. This was bank property and his possible inheritance. If Lamb died, he would have to move into this depressing box of a place.

He got out of the car, opened the wooden gate and walked up the path. An elderly woman opened the door.

6

She was bemused and tearful. She stared stupidly at him as he introduced himself.

He spent half an hour with her in a gloomy, cramped sitting-room full of heavy depressing furniture. When he finally left, he knew she thought he was wonderful and because this opinion flattered his odd ego, he didn't begrudge the time spent with her. He had learned that Lamb was desperately ill. There was no possibility of him returning to work for some months.

Back in the car again, Calvin drove slowly to the highway. He stopped just outside the town at a bar and asked for a double Scotch. It was not yet six o'clock and at this time the bar was empty. He sat on a stool up at the bar and rested his fleshy face between his hands, staring down at the tiny bubbles in his glass.

Months! he thought. He could be stuck in this dreary hole for months and if Lamb died, he could be permanently stuck here. He and Alice Craig would grow grey together. Even when she was fifty, she would still blush when a man looked at her. A fifteen-year jail sentence might be easier to bear. He drank the whisky, nodded to the barman and went out into the gathering darkness.

Macklin Drive was a mile further on at the cross roads. When he finally reached the rooming-house he was pleasantly surprised. This was a compact, three-storey house set in a well-kept garden with a view of the distant hills. Lights showed at the windows. The house looked solid and cheerful and completely unlike the other cheap little houses and bungalows he had seen in the town.

He left his car in the drive and walked up the four steps to the front door. He rang the bell and waited.

There was a pause, then the door swung open and a woman, her back to the light, stood looking at him.

'I'm Dave Calvin,' Calvin said. 'Did Miss Craig . . .?'

'Oh, yes. Come in, Mr. Calvin. Alice said you were coming.'

He entered a large hall with a table set in the middle of a fawn-coloured carpet. The lighting was pleasantly subdued. From a room at the end of the passage he could hear music from a television set.

He looked curiously at the woman who had closed the door and he felt a quickening of interest.

She was wearing a dress that had a crimson top and a black skirt. The dress looked home-made and not very well made at that. Her long legs were bare and she was wearing shabby red slippers. Her hair was anyhow and fell to her shoulders: it was brown and might have looked attractive if it had been cared for. She had rather fine features with a longish nose, a large mouth and clear glittering eyes. Her appearance meant little to Calvin, but he was immediately aware of a vital sensual quality in her that sparked off his own sensual quality.

'I'm Kit Loring,' she said and smiled. She had good teeth, white and even. 'I run this place. If you would like to stay here, I would be very happy.'

Calvin switched on his charm.

'I would be too,' he said. 'I have no idea how long I'll be here. I'm taking over until Mr. Lamb gets better. He's pretty bad from what I'm told.'

'Yes.' She lifted her hair off her shoulders with a quick, two-handed movement. Her breasts lifted as she raised her arms. 'I'm so sorry for Mrs. Lamb.'

'I've just come from seeing her . . . it's tough.'

'You must be tired. Come upstairs and I'll show you the rooms. I have two vacant rooms. You can choose which one you like best.'

He followed her up the stairs. She held herself well and she moved gracefully. He watched the movement of her hips under the creased material of her skirt. He wondered how old she was . . . thirty-five or -six, perhaps even more: an age he appreciated. He saw the wedding ring. So she was married.

They reached the head of the stairs, and she led him down a passage with doors either side. She paused outside a door at the end of the passage, opened it and flicked on the light.

'Pretty nice,' he said, 'but what's it going to cost? Bank managers have to struggle these days to live.'

'This is forty a week including breakfast and dinner,' she told him. 'The room upstairs is smaller but, of course, it is cheaper.'

'May I see it?' he asked and smiled at her. 'How much cheaper?'

She looked steadily at him for a brief moment. He felt a strange creepy sensation crawl up his spine. It was something he couldn't explain to himself.

'Thirty,' she said. 'If you are going to stay some time, I could make a slight reduction.'

'May I see it?'

The room was smaller, but as comfortably furnished as the room he had already seen. There was a double bed instead of a single one and to its right was a door. Facing the bed was a wide, curtained window.

He pointed a thick finger at the door by the bed.

'Does that lead to the bathroom?'

'The bathroom is the second door down the passage. This door isn't used.' He was aware she was now looking intently at him. 'It communicates with my room. This is really my floor, but sometimes I don't mind someone being up here.'

He was suddenly aware that his heart was beating slightly faster than normal.

'I prefer this room if it's all right with you,' he said.

She smiled: the amused expression in her eyes wasn't lost on him.

'Have it by all means,' she said, and then she looked at her wrist watch. 'I must start dinner. I'll tell Flo to bring up your bags.'

'That's okay,' Calvin said. 'I have only one and I'll bring it up myself. Can I leave my car in the drive?'

'There's a garage around the back. Dinner is at eight. If there is anything you want, please ask.' She smiled at him, then moving to the door, she was gone.

Calvin remained motionless for some seconds, then he walked deliberately to the communicating door and turned the handle. The door was locked.

He rubbed the side of his jaw with a thick finger as he stared at the door, then he went out of the room, humming tunelessly under his breath, and descended the stairs to collect his bag.

CHAPTER TWO

I

THERE were only two other guests besides Alice Craig staying at the rooming-house: a Miss Pearson and a Major Hardy. Miss Pearson, a bright, bird-like little woman in her late sixties was in charge of the local Welfare Clinic. Major Hardy, in his early seventies, was the secretary of the Downside Golf Club.

Calvin met them when he went downstairs for dinner.

The talk centred around Joe Lamb and his stroke. Calvin listened while Alice described how she had found the old man on the floor of his office. From time to time, Calvin said the right thing at the right moment, and wondered irritably when they were going to eat.

When the topic of Mr. Lamb was finally exhausted, they sat down to an excellent dinner, served by Flo, a large, cheerful coloured woman. Calvin was vaguely disappointed that Kit Loring didn't eat with them. With his ready charm and his confident manner, he easily won over the two old people who hung on his every word. Even Alice Craig seemed more relaxed as he chatted. He was careful not to embarrass her by addressing his remarks directly to her, but making sure she wasn't left out of the conversation.

After the meal, Alice went upstairs to write letters and Miss Pearson went to listen to a quiz programme on television. Calvin and Major Hardy wandered into the lounge and sat down.

Calvin allowed the Major to question him about his war record, his golf, his career as a banker until the old man had satisfied his curiosity. Then Calvin felt it was his turn to satisfy his own curiosity.

'I've only just arrived here,' he said, stretching out his long, powerful legs. 'Miss Craig was good enough to recommend this place.' He smiled his charming smile. 'Who is Mrs. Loring? What's happened to her husband?'

By now the Major, a lean, burnt-up old man, was ready to gossip.

'Mrs. Loring is a remarkable woman,' he said. 'There isn't a better cook in the district. I've known her off and on for ten years. Her husband was Jack Loring, a successful insurance agent who worked this district. In some ways, it was a pity they married. They didn't hit it off. Loring was always after the women.' The Major shook his head and paused to polish his beaky nose with a silk handkerchief. 'But that's neither here nor there. There was a child: a girl. Loring was killed in a car crash. Mrs. Loring was left a little money. She bought this house and set it up as a rooming-house and educated her daughter. She has had a very hard struggle and she's still having a struggle.'

'Does her daughter live with her?' Calvin asked.

'Certainly. She's a nice girl and she works hard too. She's in the box office of the movie house at Downside. She works the late shift.' The Major smiled shyly. 'She and young Travers, the deputy sheriff, are courting. He does the night shift at the sheriff's office more often than not so Iris prefers to have her days free. You probably won't see much of her. She doesn't get to bed before two o'clock and is seldom up before ten.'

They continued to chat until half past ten, then Calvin said he was ready for bed. He went up to his room and lay in bed, smoking and staring up at the ceiling. He never read books. Ocasionally, he would flick through a magazine, but reading didn't interest him.

He had a habit of talking to himself, and he began a silent monologue as he lay in the double bed, a cigarette burning between his thick fingers.

'This looks as if it is going to be yet another wasted year,' he said to himself. 'I'm thirty-eight. I have less than five hundred dollars saved. I owe money. If I don't do something pretty soon, I'll never do anything. I'll never be any good as a banker, but that doesn't mean I couldn't be good at something else . . . but what? If only I could lay my hands on a big sum of money! Without capital, I can't hope to get anywhere. For seventeen years now I have been waiting for the right opportunity. Now, I've just got to do something. I can't go on hesitating. Is there something I can do here in this one-eyed hole? I don't think there can be. If I'm going to take a risk, it's got to be for something worthwhile. It's got to be for big money, and I can't believe there is big money in Pittsville.'

A sound coming through the wall from the next room jerked him out of this silent monologue. He lifted his head from the pillow to listen.

He could hear Kit Loring moving around in the other room. He heard the closet door being opened and he imagined her getting ready for bed. A few minutes later, he heard the bath water running.

He reached for another cigarette. As he lit it, he heard her walk from her room with a slip-slap sound of slippers into the bathroom. He slid out of bed and silently opened his door and peered into the passage. He was in time to see the bathroom door close. Moving silently, he walked down the passage and looked into the next room.

It was a pleasant room. There was a double bed: on it lay her dress, a pair of flesh-coloured panties, stockings and a girdle. There were two comfortable armchairs, a writing-desk, a television set and a range of closets. On the wall was a good reproduction of an early Picasso.

He returned to his room and closed the door. For some moments he remained motionless, his blue eyes fixed in a blank stare at the opposite wall. Then he sat on the bed and waited.

After twenty minutes or so, he heard Kit Loring come from the bathroom, enter her room and close the door. He imagined her getting into bed. The click of the light switch told him she had turned out the light.

She was interesting, he thought. She had that something that could compensate him for the dreariness of this job and the town. He had an idea she might be easy, but he wasn't entirely sure. That amused expression he had seen in her eyes warned him it would be unwise to rush anything.

He stubbed out his cigarette, then settled himself once again in bed. He turned off the light.

It was when he was enclosed by darkness that his stifling fear of failure, his pressing need for money, his realization that unless he broke out of this rut, he would never get anywhere, crowded in on him as it did every night when he turned off the light.

He lay still, struggling to throw off this depression, saying to himself, 'You're no good. You never will be any good. You might be able to kid yourself sometimes, but you're still no good.'

It was only when he turned on the bedside light that he finally fell into a restless, uneasy sleep.

2

The next four days followed a pattern that Calvin forced himself to endure: a pattern of boredom and meaningless routine. Each morning he had breakfast with Alice, Miss Pearson and Major Hardy. At nine o'clock, he drove with Alice to the bank. The girl seemed embarrassed to be with him in the car, but there was no alternative: He lived where she did: it would be impossible for him to go to the bank by car and leave her to get to the bank by bus.

The business at the bank was dull and of no interest to him. All the time he was in the bank dealing with this financial problem and that financial problem, he was constantly aware of his need for money and the need to get away from this routine job.

At four o'clock, the bank closed. Then he and Alice completed the bank business behind locked doors. At five-thirty they left the bank and drove back to the rooming-house. Calvin would remain in his room, smoking and staring blankly at the ceiling until dinner time, then he would go down to the dining-room, eat with the other three, making polite conversation, and then pass an hour watching television before retiring to his room again.

During these four days, he got to know something about Alice Craig. She was a good worker, and once she got used to him, an easy companion. He found he could leave most of the routine work to her and he was happy to do so. He was thankful she was so completely sexless and negative. To share such long hours with her if she had been otherwise would have been dangerous. Calvin had always made a point never to have an association with any girl employed by the bank.

During these four days he had seen little of Kit Loring. He had listened to her going to bed each night, and he had got into the habit of lying in his bed, staring fixedly at the communicating door as if he were willing it to open. Each time he met her to speak to, he found her more attractive, but he made no serious attempt to get to know her better.

On the Wednesday evening while he was completing the work of the day, his desk-lamp alight, papers spread out on his desk, Alice tapped on the door and came in. He looked up, switching on his charm.

'It's about tomorrow, Mr. Calvin.' Alice said, hesitating at the door.

'Something special? Come in and sit down.'

She perched herself on the arm of the armchair.

'The money for the wage pay-out will be coming.'

'What wage pay-out?'

'It's for the four local factories. The money arrives in an armoured truck at six,' Alice explained. 'Sheriff Thomson and Mr. Travers are here to see it into the vault. Then the following day the accountants from the four factories come at nine and collect the money.'

Calvin rubbed the side of his jaw while he looked at her.

'Seems an odd way to do it. What amount is involved?'

'Three hundred thousand dollars,' Alice said quietly.

Calvin felt a sudden rush of cold blood up his spine. He leaned forward, staring at the girl, his blue eyes alive.

'How much?'

She looked startled at his reaction.

'Three hundred thousand dollars,' she repeated.

Calvin forced himself to relax. He leaned back in his chair.

'That's quite a sum,' he said. 'What's the idea – leaving it here over night?'

'It comes from Brackley. It wouldn't arrive in time if they delivered it on Friday. The pay-outs always starts soon after nine. We don't really have anything to do with it. We just house the money for the night. The factory accountants handle it.'

Calvin stared at the glowing end of his cigarette, his mind

busy. *Three hundred thousand dollars!* You could take quite a few risks to get your hands on that kind of money!

'Has this arrangement been going on for long?'

'Oh, yes, for the past five years.'

'Well, so what do we have to do about it? Are we responsible for the money until it leaves here? It doesn't seem to be a hundred per cent safe bet. Any determined robber could get hold of it. Our security isn't all that brilliant, is it?'

'It's quite safe,' Alice said seriously. 'You have the key to one of the locks of the vault and I have the other. There is also a device that protects the vault. No one could rob the vault without being detected.'

Calvin ran his fingers through his sand-coloured hair.

'That sounds like famous last words to me. Just what is this wonderful device?'

'It is an electronic eye one of the factories installed,' Alice told him. 'Once it is switched on you can't go near the door of the vault without setting off alarms at the sheriff's office and the Federal Bureau's office at Downside . . .'

'Sounds fine: so we just don't have to bother our heads? It's not our responsibility?'

'No. We lend the vault, but we're not responsible.'

'But we do have to remain here late every Friday?'

'Yes, we do have to do that.'

'And it looks as if I'm going to be a little late tonight. I have another half-hour's work to do. Have you finished?'

'Yes.'

'Well, okay, you get off. I'll lock up.'

'Can't I help you?'

He gave her his charming smile.

'Thanks, no. I have to write this report about Mr. Lamb. I'll be back in time for dinner.'

She smiled nervously at him and went out of the office. After a few minutes, she came back wearing her hat and coat.

'I'll lock myself out,' she said.

What an awful taste in clothes this girl has, Calvin thought as he got to his feet. She was wearing a mustard-coloured coat with a green collar that made her complexion seem muddy. Her big dowdy hat half hid her face.

'I'll let you out,' he said and walked with her to the door. 'Tell Mrs. Loring I won't be late for dinner.'

He watched her walk towards the bus stop, then as he was closing the door, he suddenly realized that across the street was the sheriff's office. He could see the sheriff's ten-gallon hat hanging on a peg through the big, lighted window that was half screened to hide the actual office. As a symbol of authority, the hat made Calvin stiffen and stare. He stood for a long moment staring at the hat, then he closed the door and locked it.

He remained, his hand on the door handle, thinking, then he went behind the counter, opened the door leading to the vault and descended the ten steps into the cold, steel-lined room. Facing him was the door of the vault with its two elaborate locks. He could see no sign of an electronic eye. He stared at the door for some minutes, then humming tunelessly, he left the vault, closed and locked the door and returned to his office.

He sat at his desk and stared sightlessly at his half-written report.

Three hundred thousand dollars! Was this the chance he had been waiting for for seventeen long, dreary years? The sum was certainly worth great risks, but just what were the risks?

'I'm here for at least six months,' he said to himself. 'I musn't rush this thing. I have plenty of time. I must see how the money is delivered, how this electronic gadget works. I must find out if there is any weakness in the security measures these people have taken to protect their money. If I am going to take this money, I must be absolutely certain no one will know I have taken it. That's how every bank robbery fails. Once the Federal agents know who has taken the money, you're as good as cooked. The trick in this set-up is not to let them have a clue that you have taken it. If you can do that, if you are patient enough not to spend a cent of the money until the heat is off, you stand a ninety-nine per cent chance of getting away with it. These odds are worth the risk when three hundred thousand dollars are for the having.'

With an effort he shelved these thoughts and finished his report about Joe Lamb. Then he turned off the lights and left the bank.

As he edged his car into the big garage at the back of the rooming-house, he saw Kit getting out of her car.

'Hello,' he said. 'Have you just got in?'

She was wearing a short leather coat and black slacks. She rested her hips against the fender of the car and surveyed him coolly.

'I've been to the movies. Now I must rush. It's Flo's night off.'

He came closer to her. He took out his pack of cigarettes and offered it. They both lit up.

'I'm a handy man,' he said, switching on his charm. 'Can't I help? I'd like to. I get bored sitting up in my room waiting to eat.'

Her brown eyes studied him with that odd, amused expression that slightly irritated him. It was as if she were telling him she knew his charm wasn't to be trusted.

'I never refuse help. Come on then: help me get the dinner.'

He followed her from the garage, around the back of the house and into the well-equipped kitchen.

'The menu is soup, grilled kidneys and apple pie,' she told him. 'Can you peel a potato?'

'I can make soup. Want me to prove it? What have you got?'

She opened the refrigerator.

'Beef bones, vegetables, cream and flour. Anything else you need?'

'Do fine.'

'Well, all right, then you make the soup. I'll run up and change. I won't be a minute.'

She tossed him an apron and then went out of the kitchen. He watched her go: his blue eyes taking in the shape of her body. When she had gone, he stood for a moment, his smile fixed, then he turned his attention to making the soup.

When she returned, wearing her black and scarlet dress, he was already well advanced with the soup. She collected the table-ware and went into the dining-room to set the table. By the time she had returned, he had prepared the vegetables and had set the pressure cooker on the stove. He took the kidneys from the refrigerator and was skinning them expertly.

'Where did you learn to cook?' she asked, moving to his side.

'It sounds corny,' he said, intent on what he was doing and not looking up, 'but my mother taught me. She said if ever I fell in love with a girl who couldn't cook, it would be a good idea for me to know how. It so happened I did just that thing. She couldn't cook, so I did.' He looked up suddenly, his blue eyes staring at her. 'It didn't save the marriage. I guess my mother was just kidding herself the way most mothers do.'

Kit lifted her hair off her shoulders with an unconscious, graceful movement.

'So what happened?'

'Oh, the usual thing: we begged to differ and we got a divorce.'

'I suppose I was luckier. I didn't have to get a divorce. My husband died. It's a mess, isn't it, when people marry and then stop loving each other?'

'Yes . . . it's a mess.' Calvin scooped up the chopped kidneys and put them in a saucepan. 'Have you any brandy?'

'Yes . . . it isn't much good.'

'It doesn't matter. Let me have it. I'll cook these in a brandy sauce. They'll make the Major's single hair curl.

She went to the store cupboard and took out a half-filled bottle of brandy.

He moved to the table towards the brandy and that brought him close to her. She didn't move out of his way and it seemed to him the most natural thing in the world to reach for her. His thick fingers dug into the flesh of her back as he pulled her to him. She didn't resist. His mouth came down on hers. They stood for a long moment, straining against each other, then she jerked away. They stood looking at each other: her eyes were dark with desire. As he reached for her again, she moved away, holding up her hand.

'This isn't exactly the way to get dinner, is it?' she said unsteadily. 'Are you doing the kidneys or am I?'

He drew in a long, deep breath, then he managed a crooked smile.

'I'll do them,' he said and picked up the bottle of brandy. 'You're damned attractive, but you would know that for sure.' He put a knob of butter in the saucepan and set the saucepan on the stove. 'I'm surprised you've buried yourself in this dead hole. Just why did you do it?'

She rested her hips against the kitchen table and folded her arms across her breasts.

'I made a mistake. The house was very cheap. I didn't

have much money ...' She shrugged her shoulders. 'Money! Ever since I was a kid I've wanted money. I've been waiting and waiting for money now for over twenty years.'

He moved the kidneys around in the saucepan with a wooden spoon.

'Yeah ... that makes two of us. I want money, too,' he said. 'There are people who inherit money and then don't know how to use it. There are people who even make money but still don't know how to use it, but there are also people like you and me who don't have it but would know how to use it. Tough, isn't it?'

'Then there are people who have the chance of getting a lot of money but are scared of taking risks,' Kit said quietly. 'There are people like myself who never have the chance, but wouldn't be scared of any risk providing the money is big enough.'

Calvin looked sharply at her, his blue eyes suddenly alert.

'Risks? What kind of risks?'

'Any kind of risk,' she said and smiled. 'For instance, if I were in your position as manager of a bank, I know I would be awfully tempted to steal all the money you must handle.'

He studied her, feeling a surge of excitement go through him.

'You would be making a very serious mistake,' he said. 'To take money from a bank is easy enough if you are employed by the bank, but getting away with the money is another thing. That, let me tell you, is nearly impossible. What's the good of stealing the money if you're caught and can't spend it?'

'Yes ... but if you happen to be clever and you think long enough about it, there must be some way that would be safe.'

He poured some of the brandy into the saucepan, then set fire to it. As the flames shot up, he turned off the gas.

'We're about ready,' he said. 'Will you serve the soup?'

It wasn't until after nine o'clock when the old people and Alice were watching the television and while Kit was washing up that Calvin came into the kitchen again. He picked up a cloth and began to wipe the dishes.

'You should have a washing-up machine,' he said. 'You need one here.'

'There are lots of things I need,' she returned without looking at him. 'Most of all I need money.'

They worked in silence for several minutes, then she said, 'That payroll ... three hundred thousand dollars! What a sum of money to own!'

Plate in hand, tense, he stared at her.

'What do you know about the payroll?'

'Only what everyone else in Pittsville knows about it. It arrives every Thursday evening and is lodged in the bank, then it is taken to four factories on Friday morning and the lucky people get their money.' She pulled the stopper out and let the water drain out of the sink. 'Like a lot of people, every Thursday night, I dream of that money and imagine what my life would be like if it belonged to me.'

'Have you ever imagined what it would be like to be locked up in a cell for fifteen years?' Calvin asked quietly.

She took off her apron and hung it up.

'Yes, I've even thought about that.' She stretched, arching her breasts at him. She yawned. 'I'm tired. Thank you for helping me. I'm off to bed ... good night.'

He watched her leave, then he wandered into the empty lounge. He lit a cigarette, sat down and glanced through a magazine without seeing anything he was looking for. In the room down the passage came the sound of gunfire, then hard metallic voices. There was a gangster movie being shown on television; both Miss Pearson and Major Hardy were gangster movie addicts. He sat staring blankly at the magazine for twenty minutes or so, then getting to his feet, he went up the stairs and to his room.

No light showed under Kit's door. He brushed his teeth, undressed and put on his pyjamas. Then he moved silently to the communicating door. He had no doubt that now the door would be unlocked.

He had thought she might be easy and his instinct had proved right. A woman didn't surrender to a kiss as she had done unless she was ready to go the whole way.

With a heavily beating heart, his thick fingers closed around the door handle. He turned it gently and pushed. It came as a shock when the door didn't yield. It was still locked.

He moved back, staring at the door. His blue eyes gleamed viciously, but only for a moment, then he shrugged and got into bed. He turned off the light.

He lay in the darkness, his mind busy.

So she wasn't to be had all that easily, he said to himself. Well, never mind, all my life I have had to wait. What I don't get today, I'll get tomorrow.

If I were in your position as manager of the bank, I know I would be tempted to steal all the money you must handle, she had said. Had she been joking? If he could dream up a safe way to get that payroll, he would have to have help. Could he rely on her?

Impatiently, he turned on the light and groped for a cigarette.

This was something he must think about.

CHAPTER THREE

I

A FEW minutes before half past five the following evening, Calvin came out of his office and walked over to where Alice was sitting on her stool at the counter, checking her till.

'Nearly through?' he asked, his staring blue eyes examining her.

She smiled nervously at him.

'I'm all through now, Mr. Calvin.'

'Suppose we go down to the vault and you explain what it's all about?' he said. 'I don't want to look dumb when the money does arrive.'

'Yes, of course.'

She unlocked a drawer under the counter and took out a key.

'You have your key?' she asked, getting off the stool.

'I have it.'

He followed her down the steps and into the vault. It felt chilly down there. He looked around. Stacked from floor to ceiling on three sides of the room were black steel deed-boxes: each with a name painted on it in bold white lettering. The boxes contained the private papers, the wills, the house deeds of many of the bank's customers. Facing him was the steel door of the safe.

'This is a pretty old-fashioned set-up, isn't it?' he said,

waving to the deed boxes. 'We should have proper safes for each individual customer.'

'There are no valuables in the boxes,' Alice said. 'It's all paper. People like to keep their papers with us in case they have a fire at their homes.'

Calvin again looked at the deed-boxes. There must be, he thought, over two hundred of them. The sight of them gave him a vague idea which he filed away in his mind to think about later.

'Tell me about the electronic eye device,' he said. 'Where is it?'

She pointed to a steel grill that looked like a ventilator set high up near the ceiling and facing the safe door.

'It's behind that grill.'

Calvin moved back and looked thoughtfully at the small grill. It was set in a steel frame and cemented in. He could see it would take a lot of shifting and while anyone struggled to shift it the alarms would be sounding.

'What's to stop anyone cutting the electric leads?' he asked. 'This set-up seems pretty unsafe to me.'

'The leads are cemented into the walls and floor,' Alice told him. 'There is a separate generator. It is in the safe.' She unlocked one of the complicated locks. 'Will you unlock the other please?'

He unlocked the other lock and then opened the safe door. The safe was the size of a large closet. On the floor stood a small but powerful generating plant.

'The leads run under the floor and up the wall to the electronic eye,' Alice explained. 'The eye is so sensitive that if anyone tried to get at the leads to cut them the alarm would go off.'

'Why isn't the alarm sounding now?' Calvin asked.

He saw her hesitate, then she said, 'I'm sure it is all right to tell you, Mr. Calvin. After all, you are in charge here now. I was told not to tell anyone. It is so arranged that when we turn the lights off in the bank, the electronic eye comes into operation. So long as someone is in the bank with the lights on, the alarms can't go off.'

Calvin ran his fingers through his sand-coloured hair.

'Is that such a hot idea?'

'The insurance people accepted it,' she said. 'You see, if the lights are on in the bank, they can be seen across the road by the sheriff or by Mr. Travers. There is always someone there who can see any light on in the bank.'

'What happens in the summer when you don't have the lights on?'

'We always keep a light on. It can be seen as the ceiling is so dark.'

Calvin shrugged.

'Well, so long as the insurance people are satisfied.'

Leaving the safe door open, they went upstairs into the bank to await the arrival of the money.

After some minutes, they heard the sound of a car pulling up outside the bank.

'That will be Sheriff Thomson,' Alice said and went to the bank door and opened it.

Calvin joined her.

Although he had been in Pitsville now for some days, he had yet to meet the sheriff and he was curious. He watched a tall, bulky man, wearing a ten-gallon hat and a dark suit get out of the dusty Packard. Sheriff Thomson didn't look his seventy-five years. He was still powerful, his sun-tanned face was lean and his eyes clear. He had a straggly moustache and his white hair was long. He looked like a character out of a Western movie.

He came up the path to the bank, followed by Travers.

Not over dangerous, Calvin was thinking. He's an old man and probably not too quick mentally. The other is just

a hick kid. These two needn't worry me if I decide to have
a shot at grabbing this money.

Alice introduced him and the sheriff shook hands.
Travers stood half way up the path, his hand on his ·45. He
nodded to Calvin.

'The truck won't be long, Mr. Calvin,' the sheriff said,
suddenly aware of this big, fleshy-faced man confronting
him: aware in a way that made him look searchingly at
Calvin. He thought: I don't know if I like this fellow.
There's something about him . . . that mouth . . . those
staring eyes . . . could be a devil with women.

He said, 'Any news of Mr. Lamb?'

'Nothing very encouraging, I'm afraid,' Calvin said and
abruptly switched on his charm. He had become aware of
the sheriff's scrutiny. 'Won't you come in, Sheriff?'

The sheriff was startled by Calvin's sudden transform-
ation. When this man smiled, the sheriff, like Travers,
wondered why he had been uneasy at the first sight of
him. Now the frank, friendly smile quite won him.

'I'll hang around here,' he said, then he looked at Alice.
'Everything all right with you, Miss Craig?'

Alice blushed as she said, 'Yes, thank you, Sheriff.'

They stood chatting while Travers kept watch on the
passing traffic. Then out of the gathering dusk came the
armoured truck, escorted by two out-riders.

Calvin was quick to see how alert everyone was. Although they had been doing this chore now every week for
the past five years, there was nothing slack about the operation. While the drivers opened up the back of the truck,
the out-riders and Travers kept watch, hands on guns.
Two men, also armed, got out of the truck when the steel
doors were opened. They came swiftly up the path, carrying two heavy wooden cases. They went past Calvin,
behind the counter and down into the vault.

The sheriff closed the bank doors. Alice turned the key

in the lock, then they and Calvin went down into the vault where the two men had set down the boxes on the floor of the safe, near the generator.

The taller of the two men bent over the generator. He pressed a button which started the generator humming.

'All set,' he said, and the two men moved out of the vault.

Alice and Calvin locked the vault door, watched by the sheriff. The whole operation hadn't taken more than three minutes. The two men left and the truck drove away.

The sheriff regarded Calvin with a satisfied smirk.

'Pretty smooth, huh?' he said. 'Doesn't give any bad boys much chance to grab the money, does it? You can lock up now. So far as you're concerned, Mr. Calvin, you can have a dreamless sleep tonight.'

But Calvin didn't have a dreamless sleep. He scarcely slept at all. His mind was too occupied for sleep. He told himself he mustn't even think about this thing until he had seen the whole operation. So far, providing the electronic eye really worked, he could see no weakness in the security measures. But this he was sure of: if the money vanished the Federal agents would know it had been an inside job. Suspicion would be immediately centred on Alice and himself. No one in their right minds would believe a girl like Alice with her nervous personality would ever aspire to steal three hundred thousand dollars. The limelight of suspicion would fall directly on him. It wouldn't take the Federal agents long to find out he was in debt and struggling to keep up his wife's alimony payments. They would start on him and maybe, sooner or later, he would crack. Even if he didn't, even if they couldn't prove he had taken the money, he would never dare spend it. They would be watching him all the time, and as soon as he began to spend the money, they would pounce on him.

The following morning, at nine o'clock, the armoured

truck again appeared outside the bank. From it came four accountants from the out-lying factories to collect the money: with them were the four guards. Everything moved like clockwork. The four men were introduced to Calvin by the sheriff, then with Alice joining them, they all went down to the vault while the four guards stood outside the bank, alert and watchful. Calvin and Alice unlocked the door of the vault and two of the four accountants produced keys and unlocked the wooden cases.

The sight of all that money in small bills turned Calvin's mouth dry. He stood to one side watching the four men as they counted the money, each taking the amount needed for their particular payroll, putting the money in their briefcases.

While they counted the money, the sheriff stood at the head of the stairs. The out-riders and the two guards with Travers guarded the entrance to the bank. Within fifteen minutes, the four accountants had collected their money and had gone.

During the day, Calvin continued to think about the money, but he always came back to the same impossible snag: if he took the money, he would immediately become suspect No. 1. He knew this to be fatal.

That evening, while Alice, Miss Pearson and the Major had settled down to watch television, and after he had heard Flo leave, he went into the kitchen.

Kit was pressing a dress. She looked up and smiled at him.

'Television isn't interesting you?' she asked, moving the dress on the ironing board.

'Television seldom interests me,' he said, leaning against the wall and watching her. 'Am I in the way?'

'Of course not.'

'Tomorrow is Saturday,' he said, his blue eyes intent. 'What does one do in a place like this on Saturday?'

She shrugged as she moved the damp cloth into position.

'Nothing very exciting . . . there are a couple of movies on at Downside if you can bother to drive that far.'

'Would you come with me?' he asked, watching her. 'Being on one's own isn't much fun.'

She folded the cloth and put it away.

'Thank you, but I can't tomorrow.' She looked directly at him, the irritating amused expression in her eyes. 'Besides, it wouldn't be a good thing for the local bank manager to be seen with me in Downside. People have the habit of gossiping here.'

He scowled.

'Yeah . . . I hadn't thought of that. Well, I guess I'll be able to kill time somehow. Is there a golf course handy?'

'There's quite a good one at Downside. At least, Major Hardy says it is good . . . I wouldn't know.'

'Maybe I'll take a look at it.'

She held up the dress, examined it critically, then folding it, she moved towards the door. As she passed him, he put his hand gently on her arm.

'You said the other night, you could be tempted. I have an idea that might tempt you.'

She disengaged her arm, her brown eyes suddenly alert.

'What idea?'

He hesitated, wondering if he could trust her. 'Just how badly do you want money?' he asked, staring at her.

'I want it,' she said. 'Why do you ask?'

Again he hesitated, then urged on because he was sure he couldn't do this thing alone, he said, 'I'm talking about the payroll. Didn't you say if you were in my place you would be tempted to steal it?'

She stared at him for a long moment, her face suddenly

31

expressionless, then she said quietly, 'Did I? You mustn't believe everything I say.'

'Why not? You say something . . . you must mean what you say.'

'Not necessarily.' She moved away, putting the ironing board back into a closet. 'I must get on. I have a lot to do before I go to bed.'

She was moving to the door when he said, 'Let's talk about it tonight. Will you come to my room?'

She paused in the doorway and looked searchingly at him. For a long moment she seemed to hesitate, then she nodded.

'Yes . . . all right.'

She went out of the kitchen. He waited a few moments, then he went to his room. He sat down, loosened his tie, lit a cigarette and began to think.

He was still thinking when he heard Kit come upstairs and enter her room. There was a long pause while he waited expectantly. The lock of the communicating door clicked back and the door swung open.

She came into the room, closing the door behind her. Calvin sat motionless, watching her as she walked to an armchair and lowered herself into it.

'Well?' she asked, looking at him. 'What is it?'

'You say you want money,' Calvin said. 'Will you tell me why?'

'That's not difficult. I want it to get out of this dreary town. I want it so I don't have to slave for the rest of my days. I want it so my daughter can live a decent life instead of working in the box office of a third-rate movie house. I want it so I can take her away before she is stupid enough to marry a small-time deputy sheriff with no future and no hopes of making any money. I want it to give her the opportunity to have the right clothes and right background to hook a rich husband.'

'Why shouldn't your daughter marry a deputy sheriff?' Calvin asked.

'If she does, she'll have to remain in this narrow-minded, gossip-ridden town for the rest of her days. She'll have to scrape for money as I have done when I was fool enough to marry a man who lived here. I know what it means. I'm going to take her away if it is the last thing I do.'

'Maybe she doesn't want to leave here. Maybe she even wants to marry this guy. Maybe she's even in love with him.'

Kit made an impatient movement with her hands.

'She's too young to know her own mind. Once I can get her away from here, show her how the world really lives, she won't want to marry that small-time boy.'

'Just how far would you go to get your hands on big money?' Calvin asked.

'You mean the payroll?'

Calvin nodded.

'I told you ... I would take any risk,' Kit said. 'If you think I can help you and if my share is big enough, you can rely on me.'

Calvin drew in a long slow breath.

'We'll have to trust each other,' he said.

She smiled.

'You are frightened of me?'

'Why shouldn't I be?' He leaned forward, his blue eyes gleaming. 'I don't know you. You could call the sheriff and tell him I'm planning to steal the payroll. Then where would I be?'

She laughed.

'Where would I be too? I'd never do such a thing. I've been waiting and waiting and hoping and praying that someone like you would come into my life ... a man who isn't scared to take risks.'

Looking at her, he was suddenly convinced that he could trust her.

'Okay, so you have yourself a partner,' he said. 'With your help, we could lay our hands on this money . . . three hundred thousand dollars!'

'But how?'

'I don't know – yet. It'll be tricky. I'll be the first one they'll suspect.'

'So you haven't even an idea, let alone a plan?'

'Not yet, but I now have a partner and that's important. If we are going to do this thing we mustn't rush it. When we do it, it must be foolproof.'

'I'm ready to take risks.'

'You think about it,' Calvin said. 'I'll think too. It's got to be foolproof.'

He got to his feet and crossed to the closet. He took from it a bottle of whisky. 'Let's drink to it.'

She looked first at him, then at the bottle he held in his hand. Her expression puzzled him.

'I don't drink,' she said curtly. 'I never drink.'

She moved past him towards the communicating door. He put down the bottle and caught hold of her arm. For a moment they looked searchingly at each other, then she jerked free.

'I give nothing for nothing,' she said. 'Don't complicate things.'

She went into her room, shut and locked the door.

Calvin shrugged. He poured a stiff shot of whisky into a glass.

'I'll wait,' he said half aloud. 'What I don't get today, I'll get tomorrow. She's worth waiting for.'

For the first time in years he slept dreamlessly and in the dark. He now felt secure, knowing he was no longer alone.

2

On Saturday afternoon, Calvin drove out to the Downside Golf Course.

He played perfect golf because his mind was fully occupied with the problem of stealing the payroll. He didn't think about golf. He approached the ball and hit it without bothering if it hooked, sliced or flew straight. It had flown straight. He putted in the same frame of mind. The ball would either drop or miss by yards: it dropped.

His afternoon wasn't wasted. He now had an idea. This was something he wanted urgently to discuss with Kit. It irritated him when he drove into the garage to find her estate wagon wasn't there. He went up to his room, stripped off, took a shower, then putting on a shirt and slacks, he pulled his armchair up to the window and sat down to consider this idea of his. A little after six o'clock, he heard the television start up. Then at half past six, he saw the estate wagon drive into the garage.

There would be the inevitable dinner to prepare. He would have no chance to talk to Kit for at least another three hours. He went downstairs.

He met Kit as she came hurrying in. They paused and looked at each other.

'Did you get any golf?' she asked.

'I played a round . . . not a bad course.' He stared fixedly at her. 'I have an idea. Let's talk about it tonight.'

She nodded.

'About ten?'

Again she nodded.

He went down the stairs and into the lounge. Alice was sewing on a button on a blouse. The two old people were in the other room, watching television.

Calvin dropped into a lounging chair. He switched on his charm as Alice looked up. She flushed and looked quickly away from him.

'Gee! I'm tired,' he said. 'I've been playing golf all afternoon. What have you been doing?'

She looked confused as she said, 'Nothing ... really ... sewing ...'

'Don't you find it dull living here?' he asked, staring at her. Suddenly this thin pale spinsterish girl had become very important to his financial future.

'No ... I don't find it dull at all,' she said. 'I like it here.'

'Do you ever go out dancing?'

Blood stained her face.

'No ... I don't care for dancing.'

His expression was kindly as he shook his head.

'But you should. You're young. Don't tell me you haven't a boy-friend.'

Her flush deepened painfully.

'No ... I haven't.'

There was a pause then he said, 'By the way, I meant to ask you about Mrs. Reeder's account. Couldn't we suggest she invests in something a bit more exciting than gilt edged?' Now he had learned what he wanted to know, he deliberately changed the subject. Alice immediately lost her shyness. For the next half hour, they discussed Mrs. Reeder's investments, then they were interrupted by Miss Pearson and Major Hardy who had seen the six o'clock serial and were now anxious to be entertained by the younger people.

After dinner Alice and the old couple watched television and Calvin, excusing himself, saying he had letters to write, went upstairs.

He stretched out on his bed, lit a cigarette and gave his mind again to the idea that had suddenly come to him on the golf course. The more he considered it, the more convinced he became that it would work.

Finally, a little after ten o'clock, he heard the lock click back, then the communicating door opened. Kit came in and went to one of the lounging chairs and sat down.

'Well? What is this idea of yours?' she asked, looking at him as he lay inert on the bed, staring fixedly up at the ceiling.

'Maybe it'll surprise you to learn that Alice is planning with her boy-friend to steal the Pittsville payroll,' Calvin said. 'What do you think of that as an idea?'

Kit frowned.

'I don't follow you. What do you mean?'

'You heard what I said. If the payroll vanishes, the Federal agents will know it is an inside job. Either Alice or myself will be suspected. Well, Alice is the one who is going to get stuck with it.'

Kit moved impatiently.

'No one would believe she would do such a thing.'

'That's right, but they would believe it if she had been persuaded by her boy-friend to let him have the keys and if he persuaded her to tell him about the electronic eye . . . they would believe that.'

'But she hasn't a boy-friend. She isn't the type ever to have a boy-friend. What are you talking about?'

'She's going to have one,' Calvin said and grinned, 'and he's going to be quite a boy. He's going to grab that three hundred thousand dollar payroll and vanish into thin air.'

She sat tense, watching him. 'Explain . . .' she said sharply.

'The more I think about it, the more certain I am that Alice is made for this job,' Calvin said. 'Don't forget she had both keys to the vault when Lamb had his stroke. She would have had plenty of time to make an impression of my key before I arrived. It is easy enough to do with a piece of soap. She gives the impression to her boy-friend who makes a duplicate key. She also tells him about this electronic eye arrangement. The trick of this hicky is it doesn't come into operation until all the lights are out in the bank. All the boy-friend has to do is to remove all the light bulbs except the one in the vault and then turn on the light. The vault light can't be seen from the street and when it is on, the alarm system can't operate.'

'But Alice hasn't a boy-friend and she isn't likely ever to have one,' Kit said impatiently.

'Before I've done with her, she's going to have a boy-friend, and the two of them will lift the payroll.'

'But how are you going to get her a boy-friend?' Kit demanded. 'She . . .'

'It's a trick,' Calvin said and got off the bed. He went over to the closet and took out the bottle of whisky. 'Sure you won't have one?' he asked, waving the bottle towards her.

'I told you . . . I don't drink!' she snapped. 'What do you mean . . . a trick?'

Calvin poured himself a drink, then sat on the edge of the bed.

'Alice won't know she has a boy-friend, but she'll have one just the same. In actual fact, he won't exist, but when the money vanishes, the police will be convinced it is her boy-friend who has taken it.'

Kit's brown eyes were suddenly alert with interest.

'How is it done?'

'We have only to convince two people, Major Hardy and Miss Pearson. The police will question them and they'll tell them about the boy-friend. Naturally, you and I will also have seen him, but we'll know he doesn't exist whereas the old couple have got to believe he does.'

'They may be old, but they're not fools.'

'I know . . . I know. I'm not saying this is going to be easy, but if we handle it right, it'll work.'

'I still can't see how it is done.'

'We have time,' Calvin said. He drank some of the whisky, set down the glass and lit a cigarette. 'That's the beauty of this thing . . . we have all the time in the world. So long as Lamb is out of action, I'm in charge of the bank. He's going to be out of action for months, so that gives us time. We first have to create the boy-friend. You must drop a hint to Miss Pearson that you think Alice has found a beau. Say you've seen her out with him. Miss Pearson will tell the major. They have nothing else to do but to gossip. You must persuade Miss Pearson not to speak to Alice about her beau. Tell her it'll embarrass her. They both like her and it shouldn't be hard to make them keep quiet.'

Kit made a movement of exasperation.

'But she never goes out in the evening. She sits glued to the television. How could they believe she has a boy-friend if she never goes out to meet him?'

'I've thought of that one,' Calvin said. 'You'd be surprised how much thinking I have been doing. In a few days, Alice is going to give up watching television. She's going to work for a bank examination. She's going to be in her room five nights a week. But every now and then when the old couple are watching television, Alice will sneak downstairs and go out to meet her boy-friend.'

'How will that be done?'

'We all leave our coats in the lobby. When Alice is upstairs working for her examination, you will remove her hat and coat and put them out of sight. You'll tell the old couple Alice has gone out. The proof will be her hat and coat are missing. Later, you'll put them back. The old couple will be under the impression Alice has returned. It's as simple as that.'

Kit sat motionless for several moments, thinking, then she nodded.

'Yes, of course, it could work. It's a trick, but it could work. Major Hardy and Miss Pearson will only know about her boy-friend because I have told them about him . . . is that enough?'

'No. They'll have to see him. That can be arranged. I'm giving you the bare outline of my idea. Later, we'll have to work out the details. But I'm sure we'll be able to produce a convincing boy-friend.'

Kit reached out and took a cigarette from the pack lying on the table. She lit the cigarette, flicked the match into the ashtray, then drew in a lungful of smoke. She stared at the wall behind Calvin's head, her face set in concentration.

Calvin watched her, guessing what was going on in her mind.

'Am I being stupid about this?' she asked abruptly. 'I can see we can produce a convincing boy-friend who doesn't exist. I can see he might be able to persuade Alice to help him take the payroll. I can see the police might believe this possible. But what happens to Alice? If we are planning to put the blame on her, how do we persuade her to run away? How long do you imagine it'll be before they catch her? Once they start questioning her they'll find out fast enough she had nothing to do with the robbery and there never was a boy-friend.'

Calvin flicked ash off his cigarette. His eyes became remote.

'They won't ever catch her,' he said. 'That's the trick in this. They may find her but they won't catch her.'

Kit lifted her hair off her shoulders with an impatient movement.

'Will you stop talking in riddles? If they find her, they'll catch her, won't they?'

'Not necessarily.' He didn't look at her. 'They'll find her

all right, but she won't be in the position – shall we say – to talk.'

There was a sudden tense pause. Calvin continued to stare down at the carpet, humming tunelessly under his breath. Kit became rigid, her fists gripped between her knees, her face suddenly without colour.

'It depends on how much you really want the money,' Calvin said at last. 'I really want it. I've made up my mind to have it. Nothing and nobody is going to stop me having it.'

She remained motionless. He could hear her quick, heavy breathing and he wondered if he had misjudged her. If she hasn't the nerve, he thought uneasily, to go ahead with this thing, then I'm in trouble. I could have two murders on my hands . . . Alice and she. I'm not giving up this idea just because she hasn't the nerve to help me. I'll have to find someone else, but first, I'll have to silence her.

'I think I'd like a drink,' Kit said in a hoarse, harsh voice.

He splashed whisky into his empty glass and held it out to her. He saw her hand was unsteady as she took the glass from him. She drank the whisky in one quick gulp, shuddered and sat back, holding the empty glass so tightly her knuckles turned white.

'There must be some other way,' she said.

'Okay, if you think so,' Calvin said, watching her, 'then you tell me. Once the money has gone, they'll know it's an inside job. So it has either to be me or Alice. Now you take it from there.'

'There must be some other way.' Two faint red spots showed on her cheeks. She looked at the whisky bottle standing on the night table. Calvin got up, lifted the bottle and poured a stiff shot of liquor into her glass.

'You won't have anything to do with it. It's my job to fix Alice,' he said.

He watched her as she again drained the glass.

'You'd better go slow on that,' he said sharply. 'You don't want to get drunk.'

'I won't get drunk.'

He put down the bottle, then sat on the bed.

'I've thought about this,' he said. 'There's no other foolproof way. You have to make up your mind whether Alice is more important than three hundred thousand dollars. It's as simple as that. I'm no stranger to murder. I murdered a number of people during the war ... not only soldiers, but civilians who got in my way. I have waited years for the chance of getting my hands on big money without a risk to myself. It was you who started my thinking.' He paused, then went on, a sudden edge to his voice, 'It might not be all that safe for you to back out now. You can see that, can't you?'

She got to her feet and walked over to where he had put the bottle of whisky. She poured a stiff drink into her glass.

'Are you threatening me?' she asked.

'You can call it what you like. You're in this thing now with me. Give me an idea that will keep both Alice and me in the clear and I'll listen. But make up your mind to this fact: I've told you too much for you to back out now. I'm reasonable. Give me an idea that takes care of your scruples and keeps me in the clear and we'll do it your way.'

'I'll think about it,' she said in a flat voice and moved towards the door.

'Tomorrow I'm going to persuade Alice to take the bank examination,' Calvin said. 'We have time, but there is no need to waste it.'

Without looking at him, Kit went into her bedroom, carrying the glass of whisky. Calvin heard the key turn.

He sat there on the bed for a long time, smoking and

humming tunelessly under his breath. Then suddenly, he got to his feet and began to undress.

Putting on his pyjamas and his dressing-gown, he went along to the bathroom and washed. Then he returned to his room and picked up a cigarette. He held it unlighted between his thick fingers as he looked towards the communicating door. He stared at the door for several seconds, then he put the cigarette down. Moving silently, he went to the door and gently turned the handle. The door yielded. He pushed it wide open. The bedside lamp was alight. Kit was in bed.

They looked at each other, then he moved into the room, closing the door behind him.

He felt a surge of satisfied triumph run through him. This was her way of telling him she would go ahead with him in this plan of his.

When he reached the bed, she turned off the light.

CHAPTER FOUR

I

'THE thing we have to make up our minds about,' Calvin said, 'is what we are going to do with the money when we get it.'

Kit and he were alone in the kitchen. The house was empty except for them. The old people and Alice had gone to church. Flo didn't come in on Sundays. Kit was preparing the lunch. Calvin sat on the kitchen stool, away from her, a cigarette between his lips.

'That won't be difficult for me,' Kit said. 'I know what I'm going to do with my share.'

'The take is three hundred thousand dollars. We split it down the middle . . . a hundred and fifty each.'

'Yes . . . I've always dreamed of owning such a sum.'

'You may have dreamed about it,' he said, flicking ash off his cigarette, 'but I don't think you have thought about it.'

There was a note in his voice that made her look sharply at him.

'What do you mean?'

'When we get the money, the real trouble begins,' he returned. 'We shall have all this money in cash: there's a lot of it. You realize you can't stash it away in a bank? Even a safe deposit can be dangerous. The Federal agents can search safe deposits. You'll have to be very careful how you spend it . . . no splashing it around. If you do, the Federal agents will investigate you.'

She made an impatient movement as she said, 'I intend to sell this house and leave here. With the money I get from the house, I'll be able to drop out of sight. Then I can spend what I like.'

'That's where you are wrong. It is a difficult thing to drop out of sight. But that's neither here nor there,' Calvin said. 'If you leave, then I can't. It would look very odd, wouldn't it, if we both suddenly left town?'

'I don't see why. We don't have to leave together. You could leave a few months later: what's wrong with that?'

'You are not being very bright this morning,' Calvin said. 'I am the manager of the bank. I have no other means of earning a living. I couldn't suddenly resign and leave town. The Federal agents would want to know what I was going to do: how I was going to earn a living. They would be interested especially as there has been a big robbery at my branch. Do you see that?'

'That is for you to work out,' Kit said. 'I know what I'm going to do.'

'If you are stupid enough to believe you would be safe to splash your money around you'll find yourself in trouble. In every town there is a Federal agent who keeps track of newcomers. He'll wonder where your money is coming from. He'll make inquiries and he'll find out you are from Pittsville, the town that has had a payroll robbery. He'll start checking and then you'll be in trouble . . . so will I.'

'I can take care of myself,' she said. 'I'm not scared. All I want is the money.'

'If the money is no good to you when you have it, there is no point in taking it,' he said mildly.

'Just what are you driving at?' she demanded, facing him, her brown eyes angry. 'What is it?'

'There is only one safe way for us once we have the

money. I stress the word *us*, because there isn't much point in it being safe for you and not for me since neither of us can take the money without the other. It isn't unnatural that you should think only of yourself, nor for me to think only of myself, but since neither of us can do without the other, we must think of this thing as a combined operation.'

She walked over to the kitchen table and sat on it, swinging her long legs, her arms folded tightly across her breasts.

'Can't you say what you want to say? Must you go round and round the point. What is it?'

'You and I are going to get married,' Calvin said and smiled his charming smile. 'That is the only safe solution.'

She stiffened. Her eyes showed her startled, shocked surprise.

'Oh no! I'm not marrying you! I've had one husband . . . that was plenty!'

'I feel exactly the same as you do, but it is the only safe way. It needn't be permanent. Just long enough to be convenient.'

She studied him, then because she had already learned to respect his shrewdness, she said more quietly, 'I don't want to marry you, but I'll listen. Why do you say it is safer?'

'It would be the most natural thing in the world for me, staying in your rooming-house, to fall in love with you and want you to be my wife,' Calvin said. 'We have to be sure that every move we make is a natural one. Every move we make could come under scrutiny. It would also be natural, after we were married, for you to sell this house, and for me to resign from the bank. We would say there is no future in Pittsville for either of us, which is true. We are using your capital and my small savings to go south where we hope to find a more profitable rooming-house and run it together. That story would be accepted and both of us could leave here without arousing any suspicions.'

'All right,' she said, shrugging, 'But are you suggesting we should buy another rooming-house? I'm not risking so much to get this money to be landed with another rooming-house . . . get that quite clear.'

Calvin shook his head.

'You and I will have our honeymoon in Las Vegas. It is an exciting place: a honeymoon place. I happen to have a good friend there who runs a gambling joint. I haven't seen him for years, but I know I can rely on him because he owes me plenty . . . I saved his life in the Pacific fighting. I will use some of our capital to gamble with and I'll win. My pal will see to that. In fact I'll win quite a lump of money. We will suddenly find ourselves with more money than we had originally and we will change our ideas about buying a rooming-house: instead, we'll buy a much more ambitious proposition: a motel in Florida. I also happen to know someone who has a motel to sell. We'll buy it. It isn't so much of a place, but with us working at it, it'll suddenly begin to make money. If there is one thing I can do it is to fake a set of books. We will pay, little by little, money from the payroll into a bank, showing it as profit from the motel. In three or four years, we'll have enough in the bank to let us start speculating on the market. Then once we are in this position, we are safe. You and I can part and have our money without any danger to either of us.'

'Did you say three or four years?' Kit demanded, her voice going shrill.

'That's what I said.'

'If you imagine I'm going to wait three or four years before I spend that money . . .'

'If you can't wait that long,' Calvin cut in, 'then we had better not do the job. This is a three hundred thousand dollar take. It'll put us on easy street for the rest of our lives. If we make one false move we'll both land in the gas chamber. Think about it.'

He got to his feet and left her, going up to his room, humming tunelessly, satisfied in his mind that she would do what he wanted.

Their love-making the previous night had been disappointing. He had expected a fierce, wild passion, but she had given herself to him the way a prostitute gives herself. He had the disturbing feeling that it was only because of the whisky she had drunk that she had given herself at all. He had been glad to get away from her and return to his room. It had been the most frustrating sex experience he had ever had.

It was after lunch when the old people were taking a nap and Kit was clearing up in the kitchen that Calvin had the opportunity of getting Alice to himself. She was in the lounge looking through the Sunday newspaper when he wandered in and sat down.

He said very casually, 'I've been thinking about you, Alice. Would you mind if I talked to you about your career for a moment?'

She went red and then white and shook her head, dropping the newspaper and staring at him like a startled rabbit.

'I've been very impressed by your work,' Calvin said, his voice matter-of-fact. 'You're wasted in Pittsville.' He switched on his charm. 'You should be more ambitious.'

Hanging on his words, Alice continued to stare at him.

'I – I don't understand, Mr. Calvin,' she said.

'A girl like you should be working at head office. They're always on the look-out for keen, energetic workers. Would you like me to put your name forward?'

Her eyes widened behind the shiny lenses of her glasses.

'But they wouldn't consider me,' she said breathlessly.

'Of course they would.' He paused, his trap set, then he went on, 'But you would first have to take the advance bank examination. It isn't difficult. You'd have to take a correspondence course. It wouldn't cost you anything. Head Office fixes all that.' His smile widened. 'You'd have to work in the evenings for two or three months. That wouldn't worry you, would it?'

She was pathetically eager as she said, 'Oh no, of course not.'

'Okay, then leave it to me.' He waved his big hands. 'You'll have to give up watching television, but that won't be a hardship, will it?'

She shook her head.

'It would be wonderful to go to San Francisco.'

'Fine, then tomorrow, I'll fix it for you.' Smiling, he got to his feet and wandered out of the room. It seemed almost too easy, he thought as he began to mount the stairs. Now the next move was to get Kit to tell Miss Pearson that Alice not only was going to sit for a bank examination but she had found a boy-friend.

He was humming to himself as he reached the head of the stairs when he became aware of a girl looking at him and waiting to pass. He paused, staring at her, his blue eyes suddenly alert.

The girl was fair, young and pretty. She was wearing a white sweat-shirt and white shorts. She carried a tennis racket. In that get-up, Calvin was quick to see how well made she was and his eyes ran over her young body with quick appreciation.

'I'm sorry,' he said, switching on all his charm. 'I didn't see you . . . you must be Miss Loring.'

'Yes, that's right. You must be Mr. Calvin. Kit said you were staying here.' She smiled and he saw at once he had impressed her. He reached the head of the stairs and stood aside.

'Getting some exercise?' he said as she began to move past him.

'Yes . . . I don't get much chance . . . Sunday is really my only time for a game.'

'You're working nights, I understand. That's why we haven't met.' He was loath to let her go. There was something exciting in her young freshness that appealed to him.

'That's right,' she said, waved her racket and went on down the stairs.

He turned to watch her, his eyes roving over her neat young figure. When she went out of the house, closing the front door behind her, he felt suddenly bored and lonely. He had thought of a round of golf. Now he couldn't be bothered. He went into his room, sat down and stared out of the window.

It might have made him happier if he could have known what was going on in Iris Loring's mind as she got into the estate wagon and started the engine.

She was thinking: Hmm . . . he's quite a man. He's like a movie star. That stare he had. I felt he was looking right through my clothes, but not in a horrid way either. It was rather exciting. She giggled. He is a man who knows his own mind . . . that smile . . . Hmm . . . yes . . . quite a man!

She found Ken Travers waiting for her at the Country Club. They played two strenuous sets of tennis, then went and sat under a tree where they could talk.

'Ken . . . I'm worried,' Iris said abruptly. 'It may not be anything, but I have a suspicion that Kit is drinking again.'

'Oh, hell!' Travers showed his shocked distress. 'What makes you think that?'

'When she was really bad . . . it must be over two years now, she always had a glassy, set expression in her eyes. I could always tell by that if she had been drinking. This morning when she came into my room, there was that same expression.'

'What are you going to do?'

'I don't know. I can't bear to think of it starting again after what she has gone through. I don't think I can face having that all over again.'

'But you just can't do nothing,' Travers said, his voice sharpening. 'She's done a hell of a lot for you. I admit I have no cause to like your mother. She doesn't like me and she's stopped us marrying, but at least, I have to admire her for what she has done for you. You can't let her down now if she needs help. Why not ask her outright?'

'She would never admit it. I think maybe I'll talk to Dr. Sterling. He knows what she's been through. I know nothing I say will do any good. Besides, I may be wrong. I've had it on my mind all the morning. I just had to share it with you.'

He put his hand on hers.

'Well, watch her. If you think . . . well, Dr. Sterling is a good friend of hers. Maybe you should speak to him.'

'I'll see how she is tonight. Let's get some tea. I could be wrong.' She stood up. 'I hope I am. The thought of that awful business starting again . . .'

They walked in silence to the tea pavilion. Then when they had got tea from the bar, they stood in the sunshine, sipping the tea and watching a foursome battling it out on the court nearby.

Travers said abruptly, 'Have you met Calvin yet?'

Iris nodded.

'I ran into him as I was coming out. Quite a man!'

Travers looked sharply at her.

'Yeah . . . I don't quite know what to make of him.

There's something I don't like about him . . . I don't know
what it is.'

Iris laughed.

'I know . . . he's the type every man is jealous of. He
reminds me a little of Cary Grant. He could be a movie
star.'

'You think so?' Travers grinned uneasily. 'He's not all
that good looking. The sheriff doesn't know what to make
of him either. He says he could be rotten with women.'

'There you are! Pure envy! I bet he's thrown
poor Alice into a terrible tizz. Imagine being locked up
in the bank alone with that he-man for twelve hours a
day!'

'Just so long as you don't get into a tizz,' Travers said
quietly.

Iris looked at him: her eyes sparkled.

'Is that worrying you?'

'I can't say it does. You don't get much chance of meeting the guy, do you?' Travers took her empty cup. 'Feel
like another game?'

'Yes . . . all right. And Ken . . . even if I did have the
chance, I'd still prefer you.'

He gave her a delighted grin, then linking his arm
through hers, went with her towards a vacant court.

2

By the end of the week, Alice had begun her correspondence course and a hint had been dropped by Kit to the old
couple that she had seen Alice with a handsome young
man. The old people were delighted, agreeing with Kit to
say nothing that might embarrass Alice.

During the week, Iris, still unsure of her suspicions
about her mother, had kept a close watch but had seen

nothing further to confirm her first impression that Kit was drinking again.

It was soon after Iris's seventeenth birthday, a few months after her father had been killed, that she had discovered her mother had become an alcoholic. She had returned from college one hot summer evening to find Kit sitting motionless, her face ashen, her eyes glazed, an empty whisky bottle on the table. This had been an experience that Iris was never to forget. Kit had been unable to speak, unable to move. Terrified, Iris had telephoned for Dr. Sterling who had attended the Loring family ever since they had set up home in Pittsville. He had helped Iris get her mother to bed, then he had taken the frightened girl downstairs and had talked to her.

She would always remember Dr. Sterling's quiet, kind talk in which he had persuaded her that her mother should go into a sanitorium. Kit had remained there for two months.

Iris got a job as cashier at a movie house at Downside. When Kit was cured, she bought the rooming-house with the money her husband had left her. For months Iris watched her mother. Kit seemed cured, but now just when Iris was begining to relax, her suspicions were again alerted. She continued to watch, but so far, after the first alarm, she hadn't further proof that Kit was backsliding.

One evening, a week after the first hint had been dropped about Alice's boy-friend, Kit came into Calvin's room. She received a shock.

Looking at himself in the mirror was a tall, heavily-built man wearing a wide-brimmed hat and a fawn belted overcoat. He had black sideboards and a black moustache. The sight of this stranger made Kit's heart skip a beat and she paused in the doorway, asking, 'What are you doing here?'

The man turned and grinned at her and she recognized Calvin.

'This is Johnny Acres – Alice's boy-friend,' he said. 'Not bad?' He took off the hat and tossed it on the bed, then he stripped off the crepe sideboards and the moustache.

As she watched him take off the overcoat and hang it up, he said, 'In the half light no one would recognize me. Now the problem is how the Major and Miss Pearson can get a glimpse of Mr. Acres.'

A little unsteadily, Kit went to the armchair and sat in it.

'Mr. Acres must have a car,' Calvin said. He opened the closet and took out the bottle of whisky. 'Hello! There's not much here.' He looked sharply at her. 'Have you been drinking my Scotch?'

'Is that all that of a crime?' she asked sullenly.

'Can't you buy your own whisky?' he said irritably. He poured himself the last of the whisky and dropped the empty bottle into the trash basket. She watched him furtively. 'As I was saying, Acres has to have a car. This is where we have to spend to gain. I have three hundred dollars. I'll need at least another three hundred. Have you got it?'

She hesitated, then nodded.

'I can get it.'

'Then tomorrow evening we'll go to Downside. We'll go to a movie. There'll be no secret about it. It's time the old people knew there is more than one romance in the house. Have you told your daughter yet?'

Kit's face stiffened.

'No.'

'Well, you'd better.'

She didn't say anything.

'While you're at the movie, I'll go along, dressed as Johnny Acres, and buy a second-hand car. I'll park it behind the bank until we want it.'

She said tonelessly, 'You're sure all this is going to be safe?'

His fleshy face hardened.

'I've waited a long time for this chance: every move I am making is going to be safe.'

A few days later, Major Hardy was the first of the old couple to set eyes on Alice's boy-friend. It was just after eleven o'clock and the major was finishing a crossword puzzle before going to bed. Miss Pearson had already gone upstairs and so had Kit. The major was on his own. He knew Alice had gone out because her hat and coat weren't in the lobby. In actual fact, Alice was in bed, reading *The Manual of Banking* and making notes as she read, but the major wasn't to know this. He wasn't to know that Kit, wearing Alice's hat and coat, had sneaked out the back way and had joined Calvin, dressed as Johnny Acres, who was waiting for her down the road in a newly-bought, second-hand Lincoln.

The major heard a car come up the short drive, went to the window and peered out into the darkness. He saw whom he thought to be Alice getting out of the car. He then saw a heavily-built man, wearing a fawn-coloured overcoat join her. All this he could see clearly as the couple moved into the light from the car's headlights. They kissed fondly and the major nodded approvingly. Then he watched the woman he thought was Alice run up the steps and he heard her open the front door as the man got back into the car and drove away.

Rather than embarrass her, the major remained where he was. After he heard the woman he imagined to be Alice reach the head of the stairs, he turned off the lights and went upstairs himself.

The following morning, he told Kit and Miss Pearson what he had seen when Alice and Calvin had gone off together to the bank.

'They'll make a good-looking couple,' the major said.

Reporting this to Calvin when they were alone together, Kit said, 'He has no suspicions at all. I was scared, but you were right.'

'We'll do it once again,' Calvin said. 'Next time the old girl must see us. Then we don't have to worry our heads. They'll make convincing witnesses.'

Three nights later, it so happened there was nothing on television to interest either Miss Pearson or the major. They elected to play gin rummy together.

Calvin and Kit went through the same performance as they had staged for the major's benefit, and they were aware as they kissed in the beam of the car's headlights that both the major and Miss Pearson were peeping at them from behind the curtains of the window.

'We are nearly home,' Calvin said later. He was lying flat on his bed, a cigarette between his lips, his blue eyes staring fixedly up at the ceiling. Kit sat in the armchair, watching him. 'We now have two witnesses that Johnny Acres exists. Next month the payroll is delivered on the last day of the month. Alice and I will be working late on that day. We have to get out the monthly statements.' He lifted his head and looked at Kit. 'This is the day we'll do the job. Are you still sure you want to go through with it?'

'And Alice?' Kit said, staring at him.

'Don't think of her,' Calvin said. 'I'll take care of her. I'm asking you: do you still want to go through with it?'

'You'll take care of her? It really means nothing more to you than that?'

Calvin's thin lips parted in a sneering smile.

'At least I'm honest,' he said. 'I'm sacrificing Alice for three hundred thousand dollars. She means no more to me than a rabbit that has to be killed. You, you're trying to make something out of this. You want to dramatize the situation. Do you or don't you want the money?'

Kit shuddered. Her eyes were glassy and there were sweat beads on her face.

'You are a devil,' she said. 'Yes, I want the money, but I'll never stop thinking of that girl. All right, don't sneer at me. I couldn't do it, but if you will, then I'll take advantage of what it brings.'

Calvin laughed.

'Well, that's honest. All right, so at the end of the month, we'll do it. Between now and then, we'll make the happy announcement that we are engaged.' He raised his head and looked at her. 'Have you told your daughter yet?'

She looked away.

'Not yet.'

'Tell her tonight! She has to be the first to know.'

'I'll tell her.'

'Let's go through the whole plan now,' he said. 'If you think I've made a mistake anywhere, tell me.' He let smoke drift down his nostrils while he collected his thoughts. 'Thursday three weeks ahead falls on the last day of the month. Instead of Alice and I leaving and locking up after the payroll has been delivered, we have the legitimate excuse to stay on because we'll have to work late getting out the monthly statements. As we will be in the bank while the money is there the sheriff or Travers will keep watch on the bank. They will know that as long as we have the lights on, the safe isn't protected by the electronic eye. That won't worry them because they know if anyone tries to break in to grab the money, I have an alarm button under my desk that I can set off, and besides, you can bet, they'll be on the watch. There is a back entrance to the bank that is never used. It leads out on to a small parking lot where I have parked the Lincoln. The door to the back entrance is locked and bolted. When Alice is busy, I will unlock and unbolt the door. She has a key as well as I so when the investigation begins, it will be assumed that she unlocked the door to let Acres in.' He paused, staring up at the ceiling for so long that Kit said sharply, 'Well, go on ... what happens next?'

'What happens next?' Calvin lifted his head to look at her. 'Alice exchanges that awful hat of hers for a halo. At least, I hope it is a halo. That's what happens next.'

Kit huddled down in the chair, her face growing paler.

'In other words, Alice dies,' Calvin said. 'At five minutes to seven, and you must be dead on time, you'll arrive by the back entrance. You'll put on Alice's hat and coat and we will leave the bank together by the front entrance. While I am locking up, you will go over to where my car is parked and get in. You mustn't hurry or loiter. This will be the most dangerous part of the plan, but the sheriff or Travers must see Alice leave the bank. I don't see why it should come unstuck. It will be dark. You will walk under two or three street lights on the way to the car. The mustard-coloured coat should convince either the sheriff or Travers he is seeing Alice leave. How do you like it so far?'

'Go on,' Kit said, a rasp in her voice. 'Then what happens?'

'We drive back here. The old people will be watching the serial on television. You'll hang up Alice's hat and coat. Then we'll stage a little scene for the benefit of the old people. You'll go upstairs and I'll call out, loud enough for them to hear, that you should to go to bed. They'll imagine, of course, I am talking to Alice. When they come in for dinner, I'll tell them that Alice has a bad headache and has gone to bed. You will tell them you have been up to see her, given her aspirin and she is sleeping.'

'What really has happened to her?' Kit asked.

'Her body will be left in my office,' Calvin said.

Kit stiffened, her hands closing into fists.

'You – you're going to leave her there?'

'Don't let's rush this,' Calvin said. 'Let's go through it step by step. We will have dinner. After dinner, I'll watch television with the old people and then go up to my room. I'll dress up as Johnny Acres. I'll have to walk to the bank. It'll take me a good hour. I will have left the back entrance open. I'll remove all the electric lamps from their sockets except the lamp in the vault, then I'll turn on the light switches. That will put the electronic eye out of action. I'll have Alice's key to the vault. I'll break open the boxes containing the payroll and transfer the money to one of the deed boxes in the vault.'

Kit leaned forward.

'Why do that? Why not bring the money here?'

'The safest place in which to keep money is in a bank,' Calvin said. 'They will never think of looking for the payroll in one of those deed boxes. I'm sure ... it's a foolproof hiding place. We can't use the money for some time and that's where it is going to be hidden.'

She hesitated, then realizing the shrewdness of this idea, she shrugged.

'Well, go on ...'

'Now it is your turn to come to the bank. You'll also have to walk. It would be fatal for the old people to hear a car start up. The time now will be around three o'clock. You'll have to be careful your daughter doesn't hear you leave. What time does she get back from Downside?'

'Around two.'

'Okay, I'll have to watch out I don't run into her. By the time you leave, she should be asleep, but be careful. At that hour no one should be around, but on the way to the bank, you'll have to be sure no one sees you. You know where we have left the Lincoln ... at the back of the bank. Go there, move the car close to the back entrance of the bank and wait. You'll remain in the car. You will, of course, be wearing Alice's hat and coat. I'll bring her out and put her in the boot.'

Kit took a handkerchief from the top of her stocking and wiped her sweating face. In a voice she tried to make nonchalant, she said, 'Why not leave her in the bank?'

'I want to give Johnny Acres plenty of time to get away,' Calvin said. 'We'll drive to Downside. There's a filling station on the main road and we'll stop there. I'll buy gas and let the attendant get a look at me as Johnny, of course. You will remain in the car. You'll shield your face, but I want him to see the coat. While he is filling the tank, you and I will start an argument about the last train out from 'Frisco. I want him to imagine that we're going to 'Frisco.' He stubbed out his cigarette and lit another. 'There's one thing I've forgotten to tell you. The day before we do the job, you must drive to Downside in your car and leave it in the station car park. You'll have to come back by train. We must have your car waiting for us to come back in. Got that?'

She nodded.

'Okay, after we have filled the tank, we drive to Downside and leave the Lincoln in the station car park. We'll use your car to come home in. That's the plan. What do you think?'

Kit rubbed her forehead with a shaky hand.

'It's complicated,' she said, not looking at him. 'If you think it will work, I'll do it with you. I'm no good at making plans. I've got to leave all that to you. There is one thing . . . if Alice is supposed to be running away, shouldn't she take some of her clothes?'

Calvin lifted his head off the pillow and he stared at her. Then he nodded.

'Of course . . . I had forgotten that. That's important. And another thing, there will have to be two suitcases: one for her clothes and the other to carry the money in. The cases will have to be on the back seat so the gas attendant will see them. She must have a suitcase. Do you know where it is?'

'Probably in her room.'

'Okay. That'll be your job. You pack some of her clothes and bring the suitcases in the Lincoln. The gas attendant must report to the police he saw two suitcases.'

'You really think this is going to work?' Kit asked, leaning forward to stare at him.

'It'll work,' he said. 'We'll need some luck, but that's not worrying me. We have three weeks. We must talk about it: think about it: polish it.'

'How long will it be before we can spend the money?'

'You've certainly got that subject on your mind, haven't you?' he said and grinned. 'A month after the robbery, we'll get married. Two months after we are married and you have sold this place, I'll resign from the bank. You'll be able to spend some of the money in three months' time. You'll be able to splash around with your share in three years' time.'

'You really think this going to be safe?'

He looked fixedly at her, his eyes glittering.

'It's got to be safe. If it isn't, you and I will probably run into Alice again . . . if we are lucky.'

The following afternoon Calvin had a visitor who surprised him. He was busy at his desk when a tap came on the door and thinking it was Alice he called to come in and went on working.

'Am I disturbing you?'

He looked up then and was startled to see Iris Loring standing before his desk. For a moment he stared fixedly at her, then his fleshy face brightened and he smiled his charming smile as he got to his feet.

'Why, this is a surprise. Sit down.'

Iris sat down. Calvin regarded her curiously. He noted there was a worried expression in her grey-blue eyes.

'I hear you are going to become my stepfather,' she said. 'Kit told me this morning.'

Calvin sat back in his chair. He was thinking it would be much more amusing to have this girl for a wife. She was so much younger, so much fresher and so much more sexually exciting than Kit.

'That's right,' he said. 'I hope you approve.'

'If it will make Kit happy, then of course, I approve,' she said quietly.

'I'll make her happy,' Calvin said, his charm very much in evidence.

She looked searchingly at him and he had an uneasy feeling that his charm wasn't working the way it usually worked.

'I'm worried about her,' Iris said. 'That's why I'm here. She's got something on her mind. We've always been very close and I can tell when something's bothering her. I've asked her, but she won't tell me. Do you know what it is?'

Calvin took out his cigarette case and offered it. Iris shook her head. He lit a cigarette and he wondered how this pretty little thing would react if he told her her mother was worried because between them they were planning to murder Alice and to steal three hundred thousand dollars from the bank.

'Frankly, I think she's worrying about you,' Calvin said.

Iris looked sharply at him.

'About me . . . why do you think that?'

'We've talked about you. She doesn't approve of you marrying young Travers.' Calvin broadened his smile. 'She is ambitious for you. She hopes you will marry a rich man.'

Iris flushed.

'I'm going to marry Ken, she said. 'I may have to wait until I'm twenty-one, but I intend to marry him.'

'Good for you,' Calvin said. 'As your future stepfather, I approve. I think he's a fine boy and I think you'll be very happy as his wife.'

He saw her relax.

'Have you said that to Kit?' she asked.

'Yes. I told her you should marry him. I can't see any objections, but I'll talk to her again. Don't you worry about this. When Kit and I marry, I plan to start a rooming-house in Florida. She and I will run it. I'm going to persuade her to leave you here to marry Ken. Would that suit you?'

'Of course.' She leaned forward, her face animated. 'Do you think you can persuade her?'

Calvin grinned.

'I'm pretty good at persuading people. I think I can.'

'I didn't know you planned to go to Florida. Kit said nothing about that. What's going to happen to Miss Pearson and Major Hardy?'

'Perhaps the new owner will take them on. Kit is going to sell the house.'

'When it's sold then I can get married?' Iris asked.

'That's the idea. Don't worry about it. I'll fix it. I'm good at fixing things.'

She was now looking admiringly at him and this pleased him.

'Yes . . . I'm sure you are. I'm so glad I came to see you.' She paused, hesitated, then said, 'There's one other thing . . . I don't know if I should tell you.'

Calvin stubbed out his cigarette.

'That's up to you. I'd like to think you had confidence in me. What is it?'

'You do love Kit, don't you?'

Calvin frowned.

'That's an odd question. I'm going to marry her. Of course I love her. What is it?'

'I think you should know that she is an ex-alcoholic,' Iris said. 'She's all right now, but she mustn't ever drink alcohol. If she does, the doctor tells me, she will become an alcoholic again. So please don't ever ask her to join you in a drink. I don't know if you like a drink, but if it means little to you, it would be much safer and much better if you never had alcohol in your home when you marry and settle down.'

Calvin stared at her for several long moments. He began to hum tunelessly under his breath. Judas! he was thinking, so that's it! I've gone into partnership for murder and robbery with an ex-alcoholic and she's already hitting the bottle again. Judas!

'You know it is a disease,' Iris said, a little shocked to see a sudden glaring flash light up Calvin's staring eyes. It was gone in a brief moment, but his fleshy face was now expressionless, his almost lipless mouth like a pencil line. 'It's like diabetes. So long as she doesn't touch alcohol she'll be perfectly all right. I – I thought I should tell you.'

'Yes ... thank you.' With an effort he relaxed and smiled at her. 'I'm glad to know. Poor Kit! I had no idea. Well, now you've told me I'll watch out. I don't drink much myself. I can easily do without and I will.'

Iris looked curiously at him. That brief flash in his eyes had frightened her, but now the charm was back again and she wondered if she had imagined the vicious, frightening glare.

He got to his feet.

'Well, as far as your affairs are concerned,' he said, 'just be patient. As soon as we leave Pittsville, you can marry your nice young sheriff.'

When she had gone, he sat behind his desk and lit a cigarette.

An alcoholic! The most unreliable, dangerous partner he could have chosen! And as the days dragged on towards the end of the month, he became aware that he was going to have trouble with Kit. She began to avoid him, and he guessed she was not only drinking, but losing her nerve. Whenever he ran into her, and he made a point of searching her out, he saw the obvious signs of her slow deterioration. He could see she hadn't been sleeping. She was losing weight and her complexion was becoming like wax.

As soon as he had convinced himself she was drinking heavily, he left her alone. Alice and the old couple had already been told of their engagement. Calvin now spent much of his time in his room. From time to time, he would creep downstairs and remove Alice's hat and coat to keep up the illusion that she was still seeing her boy-friend. Since he now seldom joined the old couple to watch television, they believed he and Kit were together upstairs. The double romance pleased them.

Four nights before the date set for the bank robbery, Calvin was sitting in his room, smoking and turning the pages of a golfing magazine. The communicating door abruptly opened and Kit came in. She looked distracted and ill. She closed the door and leaned against it, her breasts heaving with her heavy breathing.

Calvin waited.

'I'm not going through with it!' Kit said, her voice shrill. 'I was crazy to have agreed to do it in the first place! I'm not doing it! Do you hear me? I'm not doing it!'

'Well, all right,' Calvin said in a deceptively mild voice. 'Don't get so worked up about it. What's the trouble?'

She stared at him, her eyes glittering.

'Trouble? Do you call murdering that girl just trouble? I won't let you kill her! Do you hear me?'

'Yes . . . I hear you. If you don't keep your voice down, she'll hear you, too.'

'You are a devil! You have no feeling. I'm not going to do it!'

'Don't get so excited,' Calvin said. 'Sit down . . . let's talk about it. I thought you wanted the money.'

'Not if it means killing her,' Kit said, not moving. 'I won't have her death on my conscience!'

'There is no other way,' Calvin said. He stretched his long, massive legs and yawned. 'I told you: you haven't to do anything. I'll do it.'

'No! You're going to leave her alone. Her life isn't much, but she's entitled to it! I won't let you touch her!'

Calvin sucked at his cigarette, then released a stream of smoke down his nostrils.

'I can't do without your help,' he said. 'Think a moment . . . three hundred thousand dollars! Think what it will mean to you. A poor thing like her! Who cares what happens to her?'

'You can't talk me into this!' Kit said hysterically. 'I'm not going to do it! I can't sleep! I keep thinking of her studying her stupid books night after night while you are planning to murder her! I won't do it! I'd rather stay poor!'

Calvin pointed to a bottle of whisky standing on the chest of drawers.

'Have a drink. You sound as if you need one.'

Kit looked at the whisky, hesitated, then poured a large shot into the glass. She drank greedily in two long gulps and set down the glass with a little shudder.

'I can't do without your help,' Calvin said. 'Well, all right, if that's the way you feel, then we'd better forget it. We'll have to go on living out our miserable, drab little lives: you running a half-baked rooming-house and I the manager of a half-baked bank.'

'I'd rather live as I'm living now than have her death on my conscience.' She looked at the whisky bottle, hesitated, then poured another drink. 'You've got to leave this house. You are evil. I can't have you here.'

'We're supposed to be getting married,' he said and smiled at her. 'Remember?'

'I wouldn't marry you if you were the last man left on earth! You are to go! I mean that! I won't have you in my house!'

He thought for a moment, watching her, then he shrugged.

'All right. I'll leave at the end of the week. What are you going to tell Iris, the old people and Alice? Or would you rather I tell them that I have discovered you are an alcoholic and I now don't fancy marrying you?'

She turned white and put down the glass of whisky.

'You're not to tell them that! It isn't true!' she said in a rasping voice.

'Of course it is! You're half drunk now. It'll be interesting to see Alice's face. She admires you. It'll be interesting too to hear what the major and Miss Pearson have to say when they learn you are an uncontrolled boozer. But what should be amusing is to hear what Iris has to say.' He leaned forward and suddenly snarled at her. 'Get out of my sight. You sicken me!'

Kit turned and went into her room, closing the door and locking it.

When he heard the lock turn, his fleshy face became hideous. He looked like a savage, his face convulsed with rage. Suddenly he spat on the carpet and clenching his fists, he began to pound them on his knees.

He sat there for over an hour. When his rage finally wore itself out and his mind began to function again, he became like a trapped animal. He couldn't see any way out of this impasse. His immediate reaction was to murder Kit, but he quickly realized killing her wouldn't help him lay his hands on the payroll. Without her, his foolproof plan became impossible.

Exhausted by the murderous rage that had gripped him, unable to find a solution to the problem, he stripped off his clothes and got into bed. He lay in the darkness, his mind seething, trying to decide what to do.

Finally, around one o'clock in the morning he fell asleep. He had no idea how long he slept but he woke suddenly aware his heart was thumping. He hadn't awakened like this since his combat days. Then he had developed an acute animal sense of self preservation that had served him well. There had been times when he had been sleeping in his fox-hole, his rifle gripped in his hands, and had come awake as he had now come awake, in time to spot a Jap crawling towards him out of the jungle.

The faint light of the moon came through the curtains. He could just make out the outlines of the armchair and the big closet facing him. Why had he woken like this? He was about to switch on the bedside light when he heard a sound that made him stiffen.

Someone was in the room!

By listening intently, he was able to hear rapid, uneven breathing.

He remained motionless. His eyes stared into the darkness. Then gradually he was able to make out a shadowy figure standing at the foot of his bed. His powerful muscles became tense, but he didn't move.

As he continued to stare, the figure became recognizable. Kit, in her nightdress, was looking towards where he lay.

'Dave . . .'

Calvin slowly lifted his head.

'Dave . . . please . . .'

She moved around the bed and sat beside him. He lay motionless, trying to see her hands, trying to see if she had a weapon or not.

'Dave . . .'

'What is it?'

He could feel she was trembling and he could smell whisky on her breath.

'I'll go through with it,' she said. 'You're right. I can't face living here for the rest of my days. I've got to have money. I'll do it with you, but please be kind to me . . . please be kind to me.'

He jerked back the blanket and sheet and caught hold of her, pulling her down beside him. Her whisky-laden breath fanned his face as she twined her arms around his thick muscular shoulders.

She was crying and very drunk.

'I'll do it. I'll do whatever you say,' she moaned, 'but don't tell them about me . . . please promise not to tell them. I can't help it . . . I'm so ashamed of myself.'

His expression of contempt and disgust hidden by the darkness, Calvin forced his hands to caress her.

CHAPTER FIVE

I

'WELL, that's it,' the sheriff said as the armoured truck drove off into the darkness. 'You two are working late to-night, aren't you?'

'We'll be here until seven,' Calvin said.

'You'll be okay,' the sheriff said. 'If anyone knocks on the door, sound the alarm buzzer in your office. I'll come over or I'll send Ken. Don't open the door when you are leaving before you turn the lights out. You know about that?'

'Sure,' Calvin said.

'Then I guess I'll be getting along.' The sheriff tipped his hat to Alice who was standing by Calvin. 'Good night, Miss Craig. Good night, Mr. Calvin.'

He walked away down the path, followed by Travers and Calvin shut and locked the bank doors.

He was aware that his big, fleshy hands were damp with sweat and his muscles ached with the fatigue of three almost sleepless nights.

'Well, let's get on with it,' he said to Alice. 'The sooner we start, the sooner we finish.'

'Yes, Mr. Calvin.'

He watched her walk to her stool and hoist herself on to it. The light from her shaded desk lamp reflected on her glasses. He stood for a long moment staring at her, realizing that in less than half an hour, she would be dead and he would be responsible. He took out his handkerchief, wiped his hands, then went into his office and closed the door.

He sat down and with unsteady hands, he lit a cigarette.

The past three days had taken a toll of him. He was still not sure if Kit could be relied on. Each night after he had returned from the bank, he had found her drunk. She had been in a weepy, sexually excited state that had nauseated him, but it was essential to keep her in this mood and he had played along with her: hating her, but realizing if she was to play her part, he had to jolly her along somehow.

As he sat smoking, he began to talk silently to himself.

'This woman is neurotic and dangerous. I've got to use her, but once I have the money, what am I going to do about her? I have to have her now to impersonate Alice. I still have to have her to provide a reasonable excuse as to why we are both leaving town and more important still, why I am resigning from the bank. Without the money from the sale of the house, the Federal agents will wonder how I could afford to resign. Now wait a minute . . . let me think about this. Do I really need her for that? Suppose, after she has impersonated Alice, I get rid of her? Suppose someone offered me a good job, and as I'm getting nowhere in the bank, I decide to make a change. That would be an acceptable reason for resigning, but what if they check? I can't risk a bluff . . . someone will have to offer me a good job . . . but who?'

He sat for some minutes, his mind busy.

'Marvin Godwin . . . he owes me plenty. I was going to use him anyway in the original plan. His gambling joint at Las Vegas is a perfect cover for me to appear to make money. He'd fix it, but he would guess something was up . . . that doesn't matter. If the Federal agents keep track of me . . . and they might . . . I could prove through Godwin that I had won a lot of money. As soon as they lost interest in me, I could leave Las Vegas and drop out of sight. Working in this way, I won't need Kit once she has impersonated Alice. From the start of this thing, I had an idea I would have two murders on my hands. It could be the safest and easiest way out – to get rid of her. It wouldn't be all that difficult. She takes a bath every night. I have only to go into the bathroom while she is in there and hit her over the head and then drown her. I would fix it I would be working on my car while she was taking her bath. I could slip upstairs without anyone seeing me, kill her and then return to the garage. She would be found by Flo in the morning. They'd think she was drunk, hit her head on the taps and then drowned. With her out of the way, I would have all the money and my freedom.'

He stubbed out his cigarette, frowning. He was rushing this thing, he warned himself. First, he had to get his hands on the money which was now in the vault, only twenty yards from where he was sitting.

He glanced at his strap watch, noticing the fair, thick hairs on his wrist were shiny with sweat. It was now eight minutes past six.

He lifted the telephone receiver and dialled the number of the rooming-house. With the receiver screwed against his ear, he listened to the burr-burr-burr on the line, then abruptly, Kit's voice came to him.

'What is it? Who is that?'

From the slurring note in her voice, he knew she was drunk and his eyes gleamed viciously.

'Are you all right?' he asked, keeping his voice low, mindful that Alice might hear him.

'What . . . what did you say? Who is it?'

His fleshy, sweating hand gripped the telephone receiver more tightly.

'Are you all right?' he said, raising his voice slightly.

'All right? Of course, I'm all right. Why shouldn't I be?' She spoke loudly and violently.

'Keep your voice down,' he snarled. 'I'll be expecting you in an hour. Leave at half past six. Do you understand?'

'What do you imagine I am . . . an idiot? You've said this over and over again until I'm sick of hearing it. I'll be there.'

'Lay off drinking, will you? I don't want you down here drunk.'

'You're lucky to have me any way,' she shrilled and hung up.

He replaced the receiver on its cradle and then stared into space. He sat there for some moments, then he pulled open the top drawer of his desk and took from it one of his worn out socks filled tightly with sand.

He balanced the home-made weapon in his hand, his face expressionless, then he shoved the sand-filled sock into his hip pocket. Again he looked at his watch. He had still forty minutes before he could murder Alice.

With an effort of will, he began to work on the monthly statements. He soon found he was making mistakes, and cursing, he tore up the statement he was working on and dropped the pieces into the trash basket. He pushed back his chair and stood up. He went silently to the door. Opening it, he looked at Alice who was perched on her stool, her feet twined around the rung of the stool, her head bent as she worked swiftly and as he knew by now, accurately. He watched her. In less than half an hour she would be dead, and by his hand. He suddenly wished he could get some support from whisky as Kit seemed to be doing, but he had never been a drinking man. As he stood there, watching, Alice must have felt his presence for she suddenly turned and looked at him through the glittering lenses of her glasses.

With an effort he managed to switch on his charm.

'Going all right?' he asked, his voice casual.

She regarded him. He could see she was a little puzzled and perhaps startled.

'Yes, Mr. Calvin.'

'Good ... I won't disturb you.' He moved back into his office. He stood just inside the door, his mind plagued by uncertainty. Would Kit come? he asked himself. He looked towards the telephone, hesitating. If she had drunk too much, it was possible she might collapse on her bed and go to sleep, then he would be stuck with Alice's body.

He still had time. At half past six he would ring again to make sure Kit had left for the bank.

He forced himself to sit at his desk. His mind now concentrated on the money in the vault: three hundred thousand dollars! With Kit out of the way, every dollar would be his!

He struggled to work. The hands of the desk clock moved on to half past six. Every statement he made out was smudged by his sweating hands, and suddenly and viciously he screwed up the papers he had been working on and threw them into the trash basket.

He lit yet another cigarette, and as the minute hand of the desk clock moved to the half hour, he reached for the telephone receiver and called the rooming-house.

Flo answered.

'This is Mr. Calvin. Is Mrs. Loring there, Flo?'

'No, sir. Mrs. Loring's just this moment gone out.'

'Thanks ... it's nothing important. Miss Craig and I will be back soon after eight.'

He hung up. So she was on her way. There was no point wasting any more time. His hand moved to his hip pocket and his thick fingers closed around the neck of the sand-filled sock. He stood up and walked to the office door.

'Oh, Alice ...'

'Yes, Mr. Calvin?'

'Just a moment . . .'

He waited, aware he was breathing heavily, aware too of that same odd feeling he had experienced during his combat days when he used to slaughter Japs who he first had had tied to trees. Those moments, as he approached the line of helpless little yellow apes, bayonet in hand, had given him a sexual excitement he was never to forget. Now as he waited for this thin, spinsterish girl in her glasses and shapeless dress to come in, he again experienced this same sexual excitement.

Alice came to the door and peered short-sightedly at him.

'Yes, Mr. Calvin?'

His smile was a grimace as he waved towards his desk.

'I'd be glad if you'd check those figures. I don't seem to get them to balance.'

She looked towards the pile of papers lying on his desk and then moved forward, passing him. He pulled the sand-filled sock from his hip pocket and balanced it in his hand. He watched her approach the desk, put both her hands on the desk and lean forward over the papers he had laid out for her to look at.

He began to move slowly towards her, his eyes glittering, his breathing quick and light. As he was within striking distance of her, as he was about to swing up his arm to deal the back of her head a crushing blow, the telephone bell began to ring.

The sound of the bell went through him like a sword thrust. He remained paralysed with shock as Alice picked up the receiver, saying, 'Yes?' She listened, then, 'Why of course, Mrs. Rason. Yes, he is here. Will you hold on please?'

Calvin stuffed the sand-filled sock back into his hip pocket as Alice turned.

'Mrs. Rason is asking for you,' she said and he saw her stiffen and stare at his white, sweating face. 'Is – is there something wrong?'

He moved around her without answering and taking up the receiver, he sat down at the desk.

'Yes, Mrs. Rason?' he said, his voice strangled and unsteady.

Mrs. Rason was one of the wealthiest clients of the bank. She had taken a fancy to Calvin and he had been re-investing her money. She launched into a long conversation about a merger she had been told about. What did Calvin think? Should she buy? If she did, Calvin would have to hurry.

Calvin watched Alice take up the papers on his desk and go out of the office. He scarcely heard what Mrs. Rason was saying. He suddenly remembered he had forgotten to unlock the back entrance to the bank. Any moment now Kit would be arriving. If she found the door still locked, what would she do? Go away? Do something stupid? A drop of sweat fell on to the blotter as the high-pitched voice yammered against his ear.

'Look,' he said, trying to keep his voice under control, 'right now, Mrs. Rason, I can't talk to you. I'm sorry. We're closed. Could we discuss this tomorrow?'

'Well, for heaven's sake!' Mrs. Rason said sharply. 'I don't know what I'll be doing tomorrow. If I buy, you'll have to do something fast first thing tomorrow morning.'

Calvin could have strangled her. The startled expression on Alice's face had warned him she had noticed something was wrong. What was she doing out there? He controlled himself with an effort.

'Yes, I understand. Well, I think you should buy. I think . . .' Gently he pressed down the cradle of the telephone, breaking the connection. He replaced the receiver, knowing in a few moments she would be calling back.

He got to his feet, moved quickly out of the office and around to the back entrance. He was aware Alice had seen him leave his office, but this was too important to him to care if she saw him or not. He unlocked the door, pulled back the bolts as the telephone bell began to ring. He opened the door and there was Kit, standing in the shadows, peering at him.

'Wait here,' he said. 'Don't go away . . .'

Then Alice said behind him, 'Why, hello, Mrs. Loring. What are you doing here?'

'Answer that damned phone!' Calvin snarled at her, then as Alice, looking shocked, backed away, he said to Kit, 'Come on in.'

Kit moved into the bank. She was very drunk. He could smell the whisky on her breath.

'I thought she was dead,' she said in a loud aggressive voice. 'I thought she was bound to be dead by now.'

'Shut up!' Calvin said fiercely. 'Keep your mouth shut! You're drunk!'

Alice came to his office door.

'It's Mrs. Rason . . . you – you were cut off.'

Calvin hesitated. He wanted to scream at Alice to tell the old bitch to go to hell, but he knew he must control himself. Later, when the police began their investigation, it was possible Mrs. Rason might be questioned.

'Watch it,' he said to Kit in a low voice, then he went into the office and picked up the telephone receiver. Through the open doorway, he could see Alice was staring at Kit. He heard her say, 'What's the matter, Mrs. Loring? Aren't you feeling well?' Then Mrs. Rason's high-pitched voice blotted out any other sound.

When he could interrupt her, Calvin said, 'I think it would be a sound idea for you to take up a thousand shares. Would you like me to do that for you?'

'I guess I'll talk to my husband first. I'll call you back.'

'I'm just leaving,' Calvin lied. 'Could you call me first thing tomorrow morning?'

'Well, I suppose I could,' she said and then held him for another minute or so in an inane conversation before she hung up.

He got swiftly to his feet and came out of the office. He paused. Alice was staring at Kit who was saying in a loud, slurred voice, 'So he intends to murder you. You believe in God, don't you? At least, you go to church. Well, this is the time to pray.'

Alice looked from Kit to Calvin. Calvin's expression as he moved towards her brought a look of horror to her face. In sudden panic, she spun around and ran towards the entrance to the vault. Calvin was startled by her swift move. He went after her. As he passed Kit, she grabbed hold of his arm, jerking him to a standstill.

'Don't do it! Don't do it!' she moaned.

He shoved her away so violently that she fell on her hands and knees.

He darted down the steps to the vault.

Alice was crouching against the door of the vault. At the sight of him, she lifted her hands in a feeble attempt to ward him off.

'No . . . don't touch me . . . don't touch me!'

As he moved towards her, she began to scream. She was still screaming as his thick fingers closed around her throat.

2

Ken Travers sat at the sheriff's desk trying to concentrate on a paperback that had a naked woman lying in a pool of blood on its jacket.

From where he sat, he could see the lighted windows of

the bank. He looked impatiently at the clock on the wall. The time was five minutes after seven. The sheriff had said Alice Craig and Calvin would be through by then, then he could go to the restaurant across the way and have his supper.

He tossed the paperback aside and lit a cigarette. The previous afternoon he had seen Iris and had had a long talk with her. What she had told him worried him. He was startled to learn that Kit intended to marry Calvin, but the news went into the background when Iris went on to tell him that her mother was again drinking.

Iris now had no doubt about this. She had talked with Dr. Sterling but he hadn't been very helpful. He was getting old, and although he had promised to talk to Kit, he didn't hold out much hope.

'These cases are difficult,' he said. 'If she really wants to drink again, there's not much I can do about it. I don't think I can persuade her to take a second cure. A second cure is never much good. It's the first one that counts.'

Iris had said the old man had brightened when she had told him Kit was getting married again. 'Then that could be the best solution.'

If Calvin married Kit and took her to Florida, Travers thought, then his troubles would be over. Once Kit and Calvin left Pittsville, he and Iris could get married. Sheriff Thomson had already hinted he was thinking of retiring. Once he did, Travers would automatically step into his shoes.

Travers shook his head unhappily. It wasn't really much of a job. If only he had the chance of earning big money so he and Iris could get out of Pittsville and start a new life in some progressive town that offered scope. But without capital, he wouldn't dare take the risk.

He was still brooding over his financial future when he saw the lights in the bank go out and he looked at the wall clock. The time was six minutes after seven. He got to his feet and moved to the window to look across at the bank. He saw who he thought was Alice Craig come out and walk down the path towards where Calvin's car was parked.

Now there was a poor thing if ever there was one, Travers thought. Not that she wasn't always polite to him, but a girl who turned fiery red whenever a man looked at her bored Travers. And her clothes! He watched her move under a street light. That coat! How any girl could spend good money on a thing like that . . . let alone wear it!

Suddenly he stiffened and frowned. Was he imagining things? he wondered. As the girl crossed the street to Calvin's car, had he imagined she had lurched? He watched closely, pressing his forehead against the window pane. There . . . she did it again: almost as if she were drunk, Travers thought, puzzled, but the idea of Alice Craig being drunk was so ridiculous he immediately began to wonder if she were ill.

He watched her reach the car. She seemed to be having trouble opening the car door. He looked across at the bank and saw Calvin locking up.

Maybe she was ill, Travers thought and hesitated, wondering if he should go out and ask, but then remembering how hopelessly embarrassed she always became when he spoke to her, he decided to let Calvin deal with her.

Calvin crossed the road with long swift strides. He got into the car and started the engine. He was aware that Travers was at the window, watching him. His heart was thumping. This he knew was the most important part of his plan and the most dangerous. He wondered if Travers had seen Kit lurch as she had crossed the road. He himself had seen her lurch: would Travers think anything of it?

Kit sat huddled up in the corner of the car, crying softly and hysterically. Calvin could have strangled her. He had had to shake and slap her before he could force her into

Alice's hat and coat. He hadn't thought, as he pushed her out into the dark street, that she would be able to reach the car, but he had had to take that risk.

Now as he headed back to the rooming-house, he began to relax for a moment. As he drove past the sheriff's office, he waved towards Travers and he saw Travers wave back. Then being careful not to drive too fast, he continued up the main street.

Nothing was said until they were in sight of the rooming-house, then Calvin slowed down and pulled to the grass verge and stopped the car.

'Listen to me,' he snarled. 'You've got to pull yourself together, you drunken bitch! Do you hear me! We're not through yet. When we get in, go straight upstairs and stop at the top. I'll tell you to go to bed and you'll say just one word: "Yes". If either Miss Pearson or the major is in the hall, go past them, keeping your head turned away. Understand?'

She sat there, stinking of whisky, crying helplessly, apparently not listening.

Swearing under his breath, Calvin caught hold of one of her wrists in both hands and twisted her flesh in opposite directions. The sudden agony of his grip made her cry out and brought her upright.

'Do you hear me?' he snarled, letting go of her wrist, his hands closing over her shoulders. He shook her. 'Sober up! Do you understand what you've got to do?'

She cringed away from him.

'Yes . . .'

'All right, then do it! Make one mistake and you'll land yourself in the gas chamber.'

He started the car engine again and drove on to the rooming-house. When they arrived, he put the car in the garage.

'Come on . . . get out!'

She got out. Now she was sobering up and looking at her, Calvin was shocked at the sight of her. She looked old and ugly. Her eyes had sunk into her head. Her skin was the colour of tallow: even her lips were white.

He caught hold of her arms, his fingers digging into her flesh and hurried her up the steps and into the hall. He rushed her across the hall to the foot of the stairs and gave her a push forward, starting her up the stairs as Major Hardy appeared in the doorway of the lounge.

Calvin began taking off his coat, ignoring the major, watching Kit stumbling up the stairs. Then when she reached the head of the stairs and was out of sight, he called after her, 'Alice I think you should go to bed. I'll tell Kit to come up to you.'

He waited for the rehearsed 'yes', but it didn't come. He listened to her stumbling up the other flight of stairs to her room.

'Something wrong?' the major asked.

Before turning, Calvin composed his expression. The effort he had to make to appear relaxed brought sweat out on his hands.

'She's a bit under the weather,' he said. 'She has a bad headache and so on . . . one of these women's things.'

The major, who was a bachelor, looked wise.

'It happens to them all, the poor things,' he said. 'Best in bed.'

'Yes.'

Calvin went up to his bedroom. He hurriedly washed his sweating face and hands, then he went into Kit's room.

She was lying face down on her bed, breathing heavily. He stood over her, aware that in less than half an hour she would have an important role to play and aware that at the moment she was incapable of playing it. She was still drunk. He had to get her sober. He wanted to grab her by her hair and slap her face until she sobered up, but he realized his hand would leave tell-tale marks which the old couple couldn't fail to see.

He moved closer, then putting his hand on the back of her head, he pressed her face into the pillow. He began to spank her, viciously and violently until his hand felt burning and bruised. He muffled her screams by keeping her face forced into the pillow, and finally, after he had beaten her until his arm began to tire, he released her, dragging her over on her back and standing over her, his eyes glittering as he stared down at her.

She lay motionless, her face contorted with pain, but her eyes clear and sober.

'Are you all right now?' Calvin demanded, breathing heavily. 'Have you sobered up?'

She drew in a long shuddering breath, then she closed her eyes, nodding.

'Okay. Now get up and put some make-up on. You look like hell. I'm going down. You know what to do and say. We've gone over it enough times.' He leaned over her, his expression vicious. 'Do you know what to do?'

Opening her eyes, she suddenly spat in his face. The hatred in her eyes startled him. His hand swung back to slap her, but he controlled himself. Instead, he wiped his face with the back of his hand and grinned at her. His grip was vicious and confident.

'If you still have the guts to do that after that beating, you can go through with this,' he said. 'Three hundred thousand dollars! Remember that! Three hundred thousand dollars!'

He left her and went downstairs into the lounge.

The major was reading the newly arrived *Reader's Digest*. Miss Pearson was knitting a blue and white scarf she had promised the major for his birthday. They both looked up inquiringly as Calvin came in.

'Is Alice unwell?' Miss Pearson asked.

'A headache,' Calvin said. 'She has gone to bed. She'll be all right tomorrow. Does anyone know what's for dinner?' With an effort he switched on his charm. 'I'm hungry.'

The major smiled with the smug satisfaction of someone who has access to important inside information.

'I asked Flo . . . it's pot roast.'

While they were finishing dinner, Kit came in. Calvin looked sharply at her. Although she looked tired, there was now nothing about her appearance to attract unwanted attention. She said Alice was sleeping. She had given her a sleeping tablet. She was sure she would be all right in the morning.

Calvin broke in by saying there was a good play on television. The old couple went into the television-room. Calvin paused before he followed them.

'I'll be up at eleven,' he said to Kit. 'Keep away from the bottle . . . hear me?'

He left her and joined the old couple in the already darkened room. His mind was busy as the play ran its course.

There's no turning back now, he said to himself. So far it's working out all right. The only real danger now is if someone happens to try the back door of the bank and finds it unlocked. If that happens I'm really cooked. But why should anyone try the door? The whole town knows it is never used.

He reminded himself he would have to take a swab back with him. He made a grimace in the semi-darkness. Blood had come from Alice's nose and mouth on to his hands: he had been lucky none of it had got on to his clothes. He shrank from the thought that he would have to carry her body from the vault to the car. Grimacing, he tried to concentrate on the play. At eleven o'clock, he said good night to the old couple, saying he was going to bed, and he went upstairs. The light was on in Kit's room and he walked in.

She was lying on the bed, smoking and staring up at the ceiling. She didn't look at him as he came in.

'Are you all right?' he asked, pausing at the foot of the bed.

'You've nearly crippled me, you devil,' she said, still not looking at him. 'I can scarcely walk.'

'You've got to walk to the bank,' he said. 'Don't lie there. Move around or your muscles will get stiff.'

She didn't move.

'Leave me alone.'

'There's no turning back now. We're both in this thing up to our necks. I'm going to change. Get off the bed and move around.'

He went into his room and sitting before the dressing-table mirror, he carefully began to gum the black crepe sideboards to his face. Ten minutes later, his disguise complete, he went into Kit's room again. She was still lying on the bed. He stood over her.

'Leave here at twelve,' he said. 'Be careful. If you see any car coming, get off the road. When you get to the car park, drive the Lincoln to the back of the bank entrance and wait. Don't get out of the car ... just wait. Do you understand?'

She stared at him, her face wooden.

'Do you think I'm an idiot? Of course, I understand.'

'All right. I'll get off. Everything now depends on you ... so watch it. And keep off the bottle.'

He left her and paused for a long moment at the head of the stairs, listening. There was no sound in the darkened house, and satisfied both Miss Pearson and the major were in bed, he silently descended the stairs and let himself out the back way.

It was a fine clear night: no moon and dark. He walked

with long, swinging strides, his eyes searching the road ahead, his ears cocked for the sound of any approaching car.

He reached the back entrance to the bank a few minutes after midnight, sure no one had seen him during the long walk from the rooming-house. He pushed open the door and paused to listen. He heard nothing, entered the dark bank, closed and bolted the door.

There were ten electric light bulbs to remove. He set about removing them quickly and efficiently. The ceiling lamp caused him some difficulty. The opaque white cover was only just within his reach when he stood on the counter and the fixing screws had rusted in. He had brought tools with him and he wrestled with the screws, humming tunelessly under his breath.

From where he stood, he could look through the bank window at the lighted windows of the sheriff's office. From time to time he saw Travers pass the windows as he paced slowly to and fro. Finally, Calvin got the cover off and removed the lamp. He had been working in semi-darkness. A faint light came in from the street lamp some twenty yards away. He counted the lamps, making sure he had removed them all, then he turned on the light switch. He knew a light had come on in the vault.

He went down into the vault, entered, quickly closing the door. For some moments, he stood looking down at Alice's dead body that lay on its side, blood by her nose and mouth.

Calvin took hold of one of her ankles and dragged her body away from the vault door. He had already taken her key of the vault from her handbag. He had brought with him a tyre lever. With this, he attacked the locks on one of the wooden boxes. In less than ten minutes, he had broken open both boxes. He had already found a deed box that contained only a few papers. Into this box, he packed the neat bundles of money, until the box was full. He then put the deed box against the wall and stacked on top of it the other boxes.

He looked at his watch. It was now a quarter to one. He went upstairs and groped his way into the washroom. He soaked the swab in hot water and then returned to the vault and got rid of the bloodstains on the floor. He returned to the washroom and washed out the swab which he stuffed into his hip pocket. Going back to the vault once again, he shut the door and turned both keys in the locks. Then he picked up Alice's body and carried it up the stairs and laid it on the floor by the back entrance.

Once more he returned to the vault and looked around to make sure he had left nothing behind, satisfied, he turned off the light and went up the stairs to wait for Kit.

Part Two

CHAPTER ONE

I

JAMES EASTON, the Federal agent at Downside, a short, fat, balding man on the wrong side of fifty had begun his career in the Federal Bureau of Investigation during the gangster period. At that time, fired with a youthful ambition, he had had great hopes of a spectacular career, but it hadn't worked out that way.

In his first gun fight, Easton had learned the bitter truth that he was a coward. This, he tried to console himself, was something he couldn't do anything about. It was, he told himself, a matter of glands. You either had the right glands that enabled you to face an armed gangster or you hadn't. From then on he took every possible opportunity to avoid any kind of danger to himself with the result he was finally transferred from San Francisco to Downside and he became lost to the general activity of the Bureau, for Downside had the lowest Federal crime rate in the country.

He had a one-room office and a secretary. Her name was Mavis Hart. She wasn't pretty, but she was young, and Easton was grateful to her because she allowed him a lot of liberties which at his age he found necessary to lighten an otherwise drab existence. His home life depressed him. His wife had long ago guessed what was going on between

89

Mavis and himself and she retaliated by nagging him continually during the brief hours he was at home. Besides being inflicted with a spiteful, jealous wife, Easton had an ulcer that gave him constant pain and that frightened him.

This day, around nine-thirty a.m. as Easton was glancing through an unimportant mail the telephone bell rang.

It came as a severe shock to Easton when Sheriff Thomson of Pittsville told him that the payroll lodged at the Pittsville bank had been stolen.

Easton listened to what the sheriff had to say, his heart contracting and the flesh of his fat face sagging.

For years now he had coasted along in a dull, uneventful routine and now, suddenly, he had a major crime on his hands and he knew the spotlight of publicity would be mercilessly focused on his inefficiency.

'For Pete's sake!' he exclaimed. 'You mean it's gone?' His voice was so loaded with alarm that Mavis who was pouring Easton's two-hourly glass of milk turned quickly to stare anxiously at him. There was more talk from the sheriff, then Easton said, 'Okay, okay. I'll be right over,' and he hung up.

His fat, weak face was now shining with sweat. He was aware of the frightening pain in his stomach.

'What is it, honey?' Mavis asked.

'Some sonofabitch has grabbed the Pittsville payroll!' Easton said hoarsely. 'Three hundred thousand bucks! This is my pigeon and I'm stuck with it.'

Mavis turned pale. She knew that Easton couldn't cope with anything out of his routine. For a moment, she panicked, then she rallied to his support.

'It'll be all right, honey,' she said soothingly. 'Here drink your milk. You'll have to call the S.A.'

'I know what I've got to do,' Easton snapped. He took

the glass from her and drank half the milk. 'What a break! Eighteen months from now I'm due to retire and this has to happen!'

Mavis was dialling the number of the special agent at San Francisco. When she got him on the line, she handed the receiver to Easton.

Easton reported the robbery, trying to keep his voice steady. He listened to the crisp, efficient voice of his chief, then he said, 'Yeah ... yeah ... sure.' He listened some more, then went on, 'I'll fix it. If I need any help, I'll let you know. Sure ... yeah ... Thomson will work with me. He's a good man. I'll get over to Pittsville right away. I'll report as soon as I've got anything.' He replaced the receiver and taking out his handkerchief, he mopped his face and looked helplessly at Mavis who smiled at him.

'Don't worry,' she said. 'It'll work out all right, honey. You see ... it'll work out all right.'

He held out his hand helplessly and she came over to him, putting her thin arms around him, cradling his balding head against her immature breasts. They remained like that for several moments, then she gave him a gentle pat on his fat shoulder and drew away.

'You'd better go, honey. They'll be waiting for you.'

He straightened his crumpled jacket and smoothed his thinning hair. With an effort, he got to his feet and gave her a weak grin.

'So long, chick,' he said and reaching around her, he let his hand slide over her flat behind. 'I don't know what I'd do without you. Yeah ... it'll be all right.'

Two hours later, he was sitting in Sheriff Thomson's office. The sheriff was at his desk and Ken Travers leaned against the wall, facing Easton.

Neither the sheriff nor Travers had any time for Easton. They both knew he was inefficient, but there was nothing they could do about it. A bank robbery was a Federal responsibility and Easton was automatically in charge.

Easton was suffering from the nagging pain of his ulcer. His mind was only half on the robbery. He found himself thinking: this could be cancer. These quacks tell you there is nothing to worry about, but they haven't got this thing in their stomachs. It could be a cancer.

'What's the first move?' the sheriff asked sharply, seeing Easton's mind was wandering. 'We've got to get moving if we're going to catch these two.'

'Yeah, sure,' Easton said, switching his mind with an effort from the nagging pain of his ulcer. 'I'll talk to the S.A. It's his job to find the girl. We've got to get a description of her boy-friend.' He levered himself out of his chair. 'I'd better talk to Mrs. Loring and these old people.'

Sheriff Thomson glanced at Travers.

'Do you want Ken to go along with you?' he asked. 'He knows everyone around here and he could make things easier for you.' He gave a sly grin. 'Don't worry about offending me. If you want to work on this thing alone, just say so.'

That was the last thing Easton wanted to do. He felt unnerved by the magnitude of his task. He realized he would need all the help he could get if he wasn't to make a fool of himself.

'Sure,' he said with what he hoped was a wide, genial smile. 'You come with me, pally. We'll work on this thing together.'

Travers straightened.

'Glad to,' he said and exchanged glances with the sheriff.

Easton called the S.A. He reported what had been found out so far and he gave a description of Alice Craig.

'She was last seen wearing a mustard-coloured coat with a green collar,' he said. 'She wears glasses. She shouldn't be hard to turn up.' He then mentioned the boy-friend. 'I'm getting a description of him as soon as I can. How about getting the girl's description on the radio and television? That coat should be a clincher.' He listened, grunted, then said, 'Yeah, I'll need all the help I can get.' He felt a knife-stab of pain in his stomach and he winced. 'Okay, you don't have to tell me . . . I know it's important,' and he hung up. He looked towards Travers. 'How's about talking to Mrs. Loring?'

'The State Police are making inquiries along the high-way,' the sheriff said. 'If they turn up anything, I'll call you at Mrs. Loring's place.'

Easton thanked him, shook hands and then went out to where he had parked his car with Travers at his heels.

As they drove down the main street, Easton said, 'What do you think, Ken? I can call you Ken? You call me Jimmy. I like being pally when I'm working with guys. Do you think Alice took the payroll?'

'I guess not,' Travers said, lighting a cigarette. 'I've known her some time and she just isn't the type for a job like this. I guess it's going to be a lot more complicated than it looks right now.'

Easton drove on to the highway.

'I've been in this racket longer than I like to remember,' he said gloomily. 'I've found it's wrong to think of anything as complicated. I'm always running up against inves-tigators who make things complicated by thinking they are. Now, the way I see it, the girl has been handling all this dough for years. She has probably been dreaming what she could do with such a lump of money if ever she owned it. Then suddenly she gets herself a boy-friend and he turns her dreams into a concrete fact. He shows her how between them they can grab the money. She has the keys, she knows about this alarm system, he has the nerve, so together they grab the money. It's not complicated . . . it's human nature.'

93

Travers shifted impatiently.

'That's too easy,' he said. 'She just isn't the type to steal nor is she the type ever to have a boy-friend.'

Easton blew out his fat cheeks.

'There you go again . . . making things complicated,' he said. 'We *know* she had a boy-friend. Calvin said so, didn't he? This guy has been seen by these two old people and by Mrs. Loring. What's the point in you saying she isn't the type to get herself a boy-friend when we know she has one?'

'I know . . . I know,' Travers said. 'That's what foxes me. I am sure she isn't the type to have a boy-friend.'

Easton hissed through his teeth.

'Look, you're young,' he said. 'You haven't the experience of people the way I have. There are girls who don't look as if they know a thing. There are girls as sexless as hot-water bottles. A girl like Alice is made like other girls. She's got sex like any other girl. When the right guy comes along, a smooth crook who knows his stuff, she could be a sucker for him.'

Travers saw some sense in this reasoning, but he wasn't convinced. He thought of Alice Craig. She was so earnest, so dedicated to her work and so shy with men.

'Well, let's see what Mrs. Loring has to say. I'm still not sold on the idea.'

Easton glanced uneasily at him.

'I'm just sounding off,' he said. 'I could be wrong. You're young and smart. I need all the help I can get.'

'How did you make out with Calvin?' Travers asked.

Here, Easton felt he was on safe ground. He had talked with Calvin and had been impressed. He liked the guy.

'He's quite a man, isn't he?' he said enthusiastically. 'He sure knows his job. That's a thing I go for – a guy who really knows his job. I bet he plays a fine game of golf.'

'He's a scratch player,' Travers said impatiently, 'but what has that to do with his job?'

'It's tough on him to have this break,' Easton said, shaking his head. 'He hasn't been in charge of the bank for more than six weeks when this girl has to spring this on him. It's tough.'

Travers flicked his cigarette out of the window.

'You take the second turning on the right,' he said, 'then it's the third house on your right.'

Ten minutes later the two men were with Kit Loring.

What a woman! Easton thought. He compared her to Mavis Hart and the comparison made him feel old and unsure of himself. Looking at her, Easton realized how sordid and depressing his affair with Mavis was. To be in bed with a woman like Kit Loring would be a major experience. He scarcely listened to what she was saying. His attention was riveted on her slim, sensual body and her blatant breasts that offered a challenge from behind the soft grey covering of her sweater. This was a woman, he told himself. There was nothing skinny nor sordid about her. She had the structure and the flesh that he had so often thought about. She was the most exciting and desirable woman he had ever met.

Travers stayed in the background, watching and listening. He realized that Kit was slightly drunk and this shocked him. When she moved past him, he smelt the whisky on her breath. It hurt and worried him, knowing she was to be his future mother-in-law.

Kit was drunk enough to be very confident.

'I just can't believe Alice would do such a thing,' she said. 'Of course, this man must have influenced her. Although she is a nice girl, I'm afraid she has no character. She is very weak and unsure of herself.'

'You know for a fact she did have a boy-friend?' Easton asked, glancing at Travers with a knowing grin.

'Why, of course. I saw him. I saw them together.'

'When was this, Mrs. Loring?'

'Oh, about ten days ago. I was in my room when I heard a car drive up. I looked out of the window. I saw Alice and a man get out of the car. They kissed, then Alice ran into the house and the man drove away.'

'Did you see him well enough to give me a description?'

'Oh, yes. He moved in front of the car's headlights. But Major Hardy and Miss Pearson had a better view of him. I was on the top floor, but they saw him from the ground floor.'

Easton gave her an admiring smile.

'You tell me. I'd rather have it from you. From my experience, old people aren't reliable.'

Kit lifted her hair off her shoulders. Her firm breasts pointed at Easton who stared at them.

'He was tall and thick-set. He had black sideboards and a moustache. He wore a fawn, belted overcoat and a wide-brimmed hat.'

'Any idea how old he could be?'

'Perhaps thirty . . . thirty-five. It's hard to say.'

'You haven't ever seen him in town?'

'Oh, no.'

'And the car?'

'I didn't notice the car.' Kit glanced at Travers. His silent presence was making her uneasy. 'I suppose Mr. Calvin told you about Alice's bank examination? She pretended to be working in her room, but she would sneak out to meet this man. I knew because her coat and hat was often missing.'

Easton nodded.

'Yeah, he told me. That shows, doesn't it?' He again glanced at Travers. 'She must have fallen hard for this guy. Could I see her room?'

'Of course.' Kit led the way upstairs. On the second

floor, she paused to open a door. She stood aside. Easton, followed by Travers entered a small, impersonal room.

As Easton looked around, Kit said, 'I have to prepare lunch, if you'll excuse me. If you want me again, I'll be in the kitchen.'

When she had gone, Easton blew out his cheeks.

'Now there's a baby I'd like to drag into my bed,' he said enthusiastically. 'Some chick!'

'Think so?' Travers said, an edge to his voice. 'She happens to be my future mother-in-law.'

Easton's fat face turned red.

'Is that right? Well ... what do you know!' He looked around the room. 'Let's see what's here.'

If there was one thing Easton could do competently it was to search a room. While Travers kept out of his way, Easton searched with a professional thoroughness.

He studied the half-empty wardrobe and the half-empty drawers.

'Looks as if she took most of her clothes with her,' he said. 'No suitcase around.' He pushed the bed aside and glanced behind it. 'Hello ... what have we here?' He fished up a crumpled ball of paper and smoothed it out, 'Look at this!'

Travers peered over his shoulder. The two men stared at the letter that contained only a few lines, but they were lines that brought both men alert.

Dear Alice,

It's all fixed for tomorrow night. I've got a car. I'll pick you up at the bottom of the road at half past one sharp. You have nothing to worry about. The only thing you have to do is to leave the back door unlocked. Watch out for C. He mustn't spot you.

Love,
Johnny

Apart from the scrawled signature, the letter was type-written.

'Well, here it is!' Easton said triumphantly. 'I told you, didn't I? This is enough to put them both away for fifteen years.'

Travers took the letter from him and stared at it. So she had done it! Alice of all people!

'Yeah ... looks like a clincher,' he said slowly and handed the letter back. 'It beats me. I would never have believed she would have done such a thing, but ... well, I guess I'm convinced now.'

Easton grinned. He folded the letter carefully and put it in his wallet.

'When you've had my experience, son,' he said genially, 'you'll never be surprised at anything. Let's go talk to the old people.'

Miss Pearson and Major Hardy were waiting to be interviewed. Easton found them both irritating and tiresome. Although they agreed that Alice's mysterious boy-friend was a big man and heavily built, Miss Pearson couldn't agree that he had a moustache and the major was sure the man's overcoat was dark brown and not fawn. Also the major was indignant that Easton should even suspect Alice had anything to do with the robbery.

'My dear fellow,' the major said, 'you're wasting your time suspecting Miss Craig. She would never do such a thing. I've known her for years. She just wouldn't do such a thing.'

'Yeah?' Easton said belligerently. 'Then where is she? How about this letter?' And he pushed the crumpled letter under the major's nose.

'This doesn't mean anything,' the major said after reading it. 'It could have been planted.'

Easton turned red with exasperation.

'Who planted it? Did you?'

At this moment, Kit came to the door to say Easton was wanted on the telephone.

It was the sheriff calling.

'Just had a report from the State Police,' he told Easton. 'The gas attendant at the Caltex filling station on the Downside highway is pretty sure he saw this guy and Miss Craig around half past one last night. Do you want to talk to him.'

'You bet I do!' Easton said, studying Kit's legs as she stood with her back to him looking out of the window. 'What makes him so sure he saw her?'

'The girl was wearing a mustard-coloured coat with a green collar,' the sheriff said. 'He recognized the coat. He's seen Miss Craig from time to time.'

'Okay, I'll get over there right away,' Easton said and hung up.

He went back to the room where Travers was talking to the old people.

'Let's go,' he said from the doorway. 'Something's turned up.'

The two men went out to Easton's car. As Easton drove on to the highway, he told Travers what he had learned from the sheriff.

'You know, Major Hardy could be right,' Travers said. 'That letter could have been planted. This guy Johnny could have kidnapped the girl. The more I think about it, the more unlikely I think it is she would have done this job willingly.'

'Oh, for Pete's sake!' Easton said impatiently. 'You just said you were convinced. She fell for the guy, and she didn't have to do anything except unlock the back entrance to the bank. That's all. He could have persuaded her.'

'Maybe,' Travers said and rubbed the side of his jaw. 'But there are a couple of points that puzzle me. Where did this guy come from? If he was meeting Alice so often how is it no one but Mrs. Loring and the old people saw him? We've been asking around and no one has seen him. Where did he live? And another thing if he wasn't living here, seems odd he had a typewriter with him.'

'What's so odd about that? Lots of people cart a portable around with them,' Easton said. 'You're trying to complicate things.'

'Why did he write that letter? Why couldn't he have telephoned or seen her the day before the robbery? There's something odd about that letter. It could be a plant.'

'You've been reading detective stories,' Easton growled. 'You let me handle this.'

Travers shrugged and lapsed into silence. After a ten-minute drive they arrived at the Caltex filling station where a State Trooper was talking to Joe Hirsch, the gas attendant.

Hirsch, a young alert-looking man, said around one-thirty the previous night, a Lincoln had pulled in for gas. He couldn't be absolutely sure of the time as his watch was on the blink, but it was near enough.

'A man was driving and a woman in a mustard-coloured coat with a green collar was sitting in the passenger's seat,' he told Easton. 'She had on a big floppy hat. I couldn't see her face, but she wore spectacles. She took them off and wiped them with her handkerchief. The man was tall, heavily-built and he had black sideboards and a moustache. He wore a fawn, belted overcoat and a slouch hat. While I was filling the tank, he leaned into the car and got talking with the woman about the time of the last train to 'Frisco. She said they had missed it, but he said there was one at two a.m. and they could still make it. I happen to know he was right and joined in. I told him he could still make it if he hurried.'

Easton beamed on him.

'Would you recognize this guy again if you saw him?'

Hirsch nodded.

'Any time.'

'And the girl?'

'I'm pretty sure she was Miss Craig,' Hirsch said. 'I've seen her plenty of times in that coat.' He grinned. 'It's a coat you don't forget in a hurry.'

'How about the car?'

'It was a 1959 Lincoln: a grey job with a red top.'

'Did you notice if they had any luggage?' Travers asked.

'Yeah. There were two blue suitcases on the back seat.'

'When this guy talked to the girl,' Easton said, 'how did he sound: friendly?'

'He just sounded ordinary,' Hirsch looked puzzled. 'Just like he was holding an ordinary conversation.'

'He didn't sound threatening?'

'No . . . nothing like that.'

'How did she react?'

'She didn't say much. I heard her say they had missed the train. The guy laughed. "You're wrong, honey," he said. "We've got half an hour. What are you worrying about?" Just an ordinary conversation.'

Easton glanced at Travers.

'Doesn't sound as if she was being kidnapped, does it?' he said and winked, then turning to Hirsch asked if he could use his telephone.

Hirsch took him into the small office. Easton called the special agent. He gave him the description of Alice's boy-friend and of the car. The special agent said he would get both descriptions on the eight o'clock local broadcast and on the local television service. Easton said he was going to Downside railroad station to check further. He felt pretty pleased with himself when the S.A. said he was doing all right, even though there was a surprised note in his chief's voice.

He went out and got into the car with Travers and they drove fast to the Downside railroad station. Travers was silent. From time to time Easton glanced at him with a sly grin, but he didn't say anything.

Finally Travers said, 'This guy certainly is leaving a broad trail behind him.'

'What does that mean?' Easton asked. 'More complications?'

'Well, let's look at it. He plans to knock off one of the biggest payrolls in the district. He knows that to do that with any safety he has got to keep out of sight, got to avoid anyone getting a description of him or else the moment he tries to spend the money he'll get nabbed. So what does he do? He picks on Alice, somehow makes her fall in love with him – how he ever did that, beats me, but it looks as if that was what he managed to do. Then he is dumb enough to take her back to the rooming-house so three witnesses get a good look at him. He isn't content to remain in the car: he gets out and stands in the light of the car's headlights so he can be seen. Then he writes a letter to the girl when he could have telephoned or even seen her. He then stops for gas and has a conversation about the last train out to 'Frisco. Again he lets Hirsch get a good look at him. See what I mean? For someone with enough ambition to steal three hundred thousand dollars, he doesn't seem to me to be a major mind.'

'Who said he was a major mind?' Easton asked irritably. It's because the average crook is a born dope that he gets caught.'

'I'm not so sure this guy is a dope,' Travers said. 'Those sideboards and the moustache could be a good disguise. It's my bet, he wanted to be seen so we'd get a wrong description of him. We're looking for a man with sideboards. If he takes them off, we haven't a description of him at all.'

'Maybe,' Easton said, a little startled, 'but we have a description of the girl. Where she is, he is.'

'I'm worrying about her,' Travers said soberly.

'What does that mean?'

'I don't know . . . but I'm worrying just the same.'

Easton shrugged his fat shoulders and drove on in silence.

When they reached the railroad station, Easton spent some time talking to the staff. Both the ticket officer and the ticket puncher were sure no one had boarded the two a.m. train to San Francisco. Nor had they seen anyone resembling Johnny nor any woman in a mustard-coloured coat.

Realizing that the trail that had appeared so hot was now cold, Easton walked dejectedly back to his car.

'So they didn't take the train to 'Frisco,' he said. 'I've got to get to a telephone. I must talk to the S.A.'

'There's a booth across the way,' Travers said and got into the car. He watched Easton plod across the road and shut himself in the booth. After a while he finished talking with the S.A. and joined Travers.

'I guess we'd better go back to Pittsville and wait for something to break after the broadcast,' he said. 'The S.A. is sending a bunch of boys to take the town apart. We've got to get a lead on this Johnny. It'll mean a house-to-house check.'

Travers didn't say anything.

They drove back to Pittsville.

2

Calvin was glad to close the bank for the lunch recess. Single-handed, he had had a very busy morning. The news of the robbery had brought many people to the bank ostensibly to cash small cheques but really to get first-hand information from Calvin.

When he had finally persuaded the last customer to leave, and after he had locked the doors, he went into his office and lit a cigarette. Everything was working out the way he planned, but for all that he was uneasy. He was worried about Kit. He hadn't seen her since the previous night and he was wondering how she was reacting. He was sure by now that Easton had talked with her. Although he was tempted to telephone her to find out what had taken place, he resisted the impulse. Any moment now, the auditors from head office would be arriving to make a complete bank audit. Calvin had been asked if he couldn't find some local girl to take Alice's place as there was no one at head office who could be spared. This had given Calvin an idea. He reached for the telephone and called the rooming-house. Flo answered.

'Is Miss Iris in?' Calvin asked. 'Could I speak to her?'

Flo said Iris was just about to go out, but to hold on. A moment later Iris's young, fresh voice came over the line.

'Hello there,' Calvin said. 'If you're passing the bank, could you look in? There's something I want to talk to you about.'

'I'll be passing in about half an hour,' Iris said, her voice revealing her surprise. 'What is it?'

'Something I'd rather not talk about over the telephone,' Calvin returned, and he hung up.

When he had broken the connection he called the snack-bar across the road and told them to send over a couple of chicken sandwiches. Then getting to his feet, he went down into the vault. He stood looking at the deed box in which he had hidden the money. The box stood on the floor with some twenty other boxes on top of it. Calvin's fleshy face lit up as he thought of the money in the box and he longed to open the box and finger the neat packets of money, but he resisted the impulse.

He left the vault and hearing a rapping on the bank door, he opened up and took the sandwiches from the boy the snack-bar had sent over. He tipped the boy, relocked the bank door and returned to his office. He began to eat the sandwiches.

As he was about to start on the second sandwich, he heard rapping on the bank door again and he opened it.

Iris looked inquiringly at him. She was wearing a sports shirt and a pleated white skirt. Calvin felt a sudden stab of desire run through him as his eyes took in her young, well-developed body.

'Come on in,' he said, his smile wide and charming. 'What a morning I've had! I'm just snatching lunch. Phew! Everyone's been in making sure they haven't lost their money!'

Iris walked past him into the bank and turned to watch him shut and lock the door.

'You must have had a time,' she said sympathetically. 'I've been listening to the radio nearly all the morning.'

Calvin led the way into his office.

'Yes ... it's been pretty rugged.' He waved her to the visitor's chair and then going around his desk, he sat down. 'Alice of all people! I don't know ... It's a shock.'

Iris stiffened.

'You don't really believe she took the money, do you?'

'Well, she's gone and the money's gone.'

'I was talking to Ken on the telephone this morning. He thinks she was forced to do it and has been kidnapped.'

This news startled Calvin.

'That's an angle I hadn't thought of ... could be he's right. It makes sense. Alice just isn't the type to steal. Did he say what was happening?'

'They are making a house-to-house check to try to find

this man or at least where he stayed when he was seeing Alice. They're hunting for Alice, too, of course.'

Calvin picked up the half-eaten sandwich and bit into it.

'There's something I want to talk to you about,' he said. 'I'm now short of an assistant. I must have someone here to help me. Head Office has told me to find local talent.' He smiled at her, watching her intently. 'I thought of you. Would you be interested to work here? The pay isn't bad ... seventy-five a week.'

She looked surprised.

'But I don't know a thing about banking.'

'You don't have to. There's some typing to do and the rest you can easily pick up.' He wiped his fingers on his handkerchief, watching her. 'I'd like my future daughter-in-law to work with me. I wish you would. There's no future in working for a movie house. What do you say?'

She hesitated.

'I've been working night shifts so I could see Ken,' she said. 'I don't know how he will react.'

'He's going to be busy on this robbery,' Calvin said. 'Besides, it isn't good to work at night. Come on, let me persuade you.'

She suddenly smiled.

'Yes, all right. I'd like to.'

Calvin nodded, pleased.

'Fine. Look, I'm under pressure. Do you think you could start tomorrow? If you have to lose your salary at the movie house, the bank will make it up to you.'

'Yes ... all right, I'll start tomorrow.'

He got to his feet.

'I have the auditors coming and I must be ready for them. We'll make a start tomorrow. I'll drive you in as I used to drive poor Alice.'

They walked to the door together.

'Kit all right?' Calvin asked as he unlocked the bank door. 'I didn't see her this morning.'

'I haven't either.' Iris said, her face clouding. 'She worries me. She seems to be avoiding me. I haven't seen her to talk to more than three or four times during the past week.'

'You musn't worry about her,' Calvin said. 'She's all right. I see her every evening. I think she's a little unsettled about getting married again. It's understandable.' He paused, then went on, 'I can imagine what you are thinking. You're worried about her drinking. Well, I've talked to her. She admitted she had started again, but she's promised to stop. It'll be all right. I'm going to look after her.'

'That's a relief!' Iris said. 'I certainly was worrying about that.'

'Well, don't. I've got all that taken care of. Now I must get back to work. I look forward to working with you tomorrow.' He gave her his charming smile and then closed the bank door after her.

He walked heavy-footed back to his office. He picked up the telephone receiver and dialled the number of the rooming-house. When Flo came on the line, he asked if he could speak to Kit.

Flo sounded worried.

'Miss Kit ain't down yet, Mr. Calvin, sir,' she said. 'I've been up to her room, but she says I'm not to disturb her. Should I go up again?'

'No ... leave it,' Calvin said. 'You carry on, Flo. I expect she's upset about Miss Alice,' and he hung up.

His fleshy face twisted with rage.

She was drunk again. He would have to get rid of her. The sooner the better. She was dangerous.

Yes, he would have to get rid of her.

CHAPTER TWO

I

EASTON, Sheriff Thomson and Travers sat in the sheriff's office. The time was twenty minutes past eight p.m. Easton was sipping a glass of milk. The sheriff and Travers were drinking beer. They had listened to the eight o'clock broadcast, giving a description of Johnny and of the Lincoln car.

The sudden sound of the telephone bell brought the three men alert.

'Here we go,' the sheriff said and reached for the telephone. He listened to a man's voice that came over the line.

'Okay, Mr. Oakes,' he said. 'Sure, I've got it. We'll be right over if you'll wait for us. Yeah ... say in thirty minutes.' He hung up and looked at Easton, 'Oakes of Triumph Car Mart at Downside. He's pretty sure he sold the Lincoln to our friend.'

Easton finished his milk and stood up.

'You stick here, sheriff, in case any more leads come in. Ken and me will go see this guy.'

Thirty minutes later, Easton and Travers walked into the brightly lit car mart.

Seeing them come, Fred Oakes, a fat, elderly man, hurried towards them.

After introductions, he said, 'This fella matched the description I heard on the radio. He was tall, heavily built and he had black sideboards and a moustache. He wore a belted, fawn-coloured coat.'

'Just when did you see him, Mr. Oakes?' Easton asked.

'I've got the exact date and the time,' Oakes said. 'I have it right here for you, together with the fella's address.' He gave Easton a copy of the sale receipt of the Lincoln, bearing an address.

Easton scratched the side of his neck as he stared at the address.

'Johnny Acres, 12477, California Drive, Los Angeles,' he intoned. 'Probably phoney. Anyway, I'll check.' He looked at Oakes, 'Could you identify this man again?'

Fred Oakes nodded. Although his feet ached and he was tired, he was enjoying being questioned. He knew for sure he would see his name in the papers the following day: maybe, even a photograph.

'I'd know him anywhere.'

'Was he alone?'

'Yes.'

'How did he pay?'

'In cash. He gave me sixty ten-dollar bills.'

'Any chance of examining the bills?'

Oakes shook his head.

'We do most of our business in cash. The money's been banked days ago.'

Travers asked, 'Mr. Oakes, how did you react to this man – as a man? Did you like him?'

Oakes was quick to understand what Travers meant.

'I couldn't say I took to him. I didn't pay much attention to him, but I got the impression he wasn't the sort of guy you'd pick for a friend. I can't say why. There was something about him ... then he had this habit of humming under his breath. It irritated me.'

Travers became alert.

'Humming under his breath?'

'That's right. Whenever I was talking to him, he started this low humming sound . . . sort of an unconscious habit I guess.'

Easton said impatiently, 'Never mind that stuff, let's have the details of the car. I want the licence number, the engine number and the make of tyres.'

Oakes supplied the information and Easton jotted it down. Then shaking Oakes's hand, Easton got back into his car.

'Well, here's something for the S.A. to work on,' he said as Travers joined him. 'We should be able to pick up the car pretty fast. I'm going back to the office. What do you want to do?'

'Drop me off at the station,' Travers said. 'I'll take a train back.'

As Easton headed for the station, he said, 'We've got to find out where this guy kept the Lincoln. He bought it nearly a month ago. He must have kept it somewhere. I'll have the S.A. put out another broadcast.'

'He could have left it in one of the big parking lots at Downside,' Travers said. 'No one would notice it. The parking lot by the railroad station has cars on it night and day. He could have left it there.'

'Yeah, I guess that's right.'

'You'll tell the S.A. about this guy's habit of humming under his breath? He might be on record,' Travers said. 'The sideboards and the moustache can be removed, but when you have an unconscious habit like that, you don't lose it.'

'I'll tell him,' Easton said grudgingly, 'but I don't reckon somehow he's an old-timer.'

He pulled up outside the station.

'See you tomorrow,' Travers said, getting out. 'Will you be over?'

'I guess so,' Easton returned and with a wave of his hand, he started the car.

'Hey! Wait!' Travers yelled.

Easton pulled up and peered out of the car window. Travers was staring across at the vast car park. The light was failing, but his sharp eyes had spotted a car that aroused his attention.

'Look at that Lincoln,' he said, pointing. 'A red top and a grey body. Could be the one we want. The third car in the second row.'

Easton scrambled out of his car and peered into the gloom.

'Damned if I can see it,' he muttered, then as Travers started towards the parking lot, he joined him. They paused finally beside the Lincoln.

'It's the one!' Travers said. 'Look ... the licence number!'

'What a break!' Easton said excitedly.

'We'd better get it towed to headquarters,' Travers said. 'The boys will want to go over it. I'll wait here if you'll get a wrecking crew.'

Easton hurried over to the telephone booth by the railroad station and called the Downside Police Headquarters.

While Travers waited, he peered through the windows of the locked car, shining his torch on to the empty seats.

Easton returned.

'They're coming right away,' he said. 'Maybe we'll get his prints.'

'I bet we don't,' Travers returned. 'I'm beginning to respect Mr. Acres. He's playing it smart. He leaves a trail a mile wide to the station by talking about the 'Frisco train, then he leaves his car right here for us to find. I have an idea he could still be in the district.'

Easton pushed his hat to the back of his head and wiped his forehead.

'You keep sounding off about this guy,' he said, 'but how's about the girl? They're in this together, aren't they?'

'For her sake, I hope so.'

'What does that mean?' Easton asked, staring. 'Don't let's get this thing complicated. It's bad enough the way it is without adding to our troubles.'

Ten minutes later, the wrecking crew arrived and towed the Lincoln to police headquarters.

Easton and Travers stood under an arc lamp while three detectives began a systematic examination of the car.

It wasn't until they opened the boot that they found Alice's body.

It came as no surprise to Travers. He had been sure, when eventually she was found, Alice would be dead.

2

Calvin didn't get back to the rooming-house until after eight o'clock. The auditors had worked late, and he had been obliged to hang around until they finally decided to leave the rest of the work until the following day.

He opened the front door silently. He could hear the familiar sound of the television and guessed that Major Hardy and Miss Pearson had settled down to their evening soporific entertainment.

He had had a snack dinner with the auditors and he was now feeling relaxed. He moved quietly up the stairs to his room. Closing the door, he took off his coat, ripped off his tie and sank into the armchair.

He was pleased that his nerves were so steady. It had

been an anxious day, but he had weathered it, and now, he began to wonder what progress Easton had made.

When Easton had called on him, Calvin had quickly realized that this man needn't worry him. He had expected much sterner opposition. The sight of the short, fat, balding agent had done much to calm Calvin's jumping nerves and restore his confidence. But he was aware that although Easton appeared inefficient, Ken Travers had to be reckoned with. This young man was smart, alert and ambitious. He would be the one to watch.

Calvin lit a cigarette. Then he reached out, opened the closet by him and took out the bottle of whisky. It was empty.

For a long moment he stared at the bottle, his face suddenly vicious, his eyes glaring. This morning it had been almost full. He could guess who had been drinking his liquor.

'She's got to go,' he said, half aloud. 'I can't afford to let her live, the drunken bitch. Why wait? I'll get rid of her tonight. With all that whisky inside her, they'll think she had a fainting fit and drowned herself. I'll do it tonight.'

He got slowly to his feet and walked across the room to the communicating door. He opened the door and walked into Kit's room.

Kit was lying on the bed. She had on a blue nylon wrap that had fallen open to show her long, slim legs. She half raised her head to look at him.

'Hello, murderer,' she said. 'I'm surprised you want to see me. How do you like living with yourself now?'

He came in and shut the door, then moving to the foot of the bed, he stared at her.

'What's bothering you?' she asked, her brown eyes glittering unnaturally. 'Not your conscience, I'm sure.'

'Did you see Easton?' Calvin asked in a deceptively mild voice.

'I did. He's not worrying you, is he? A fat, lecherous fool. All he could think about and stare at was my body.'

'Sure?' Calvin's thin lips twisted into a sneer. 'I admit he isn't much, but maybe he was thinking a drunk is an easy lay.'

Her face tightened with sudden fury.

'What do you want? Say what you want and get out!'

'I've found a replacement for Alice,' Calvin said, moving to an armchair and sitting down. 'I thought you would be interested.'

She half raised herself, resting her weight on her arm.

'Why should I be? What new devilment is going on in that filthy mind of yours?'

Calvin smiled his charming smile.

'You haven't seen Iris today?'

She stiffened, her eyes narrowing.

'What do you mean?'

'She came to the bank this morning. She's worried about you. She says you have been avoiding her recently.'

Kit swung her legs off the bed and sat up. Her eyes were pools of fear and anger.

'I won't have you discussing me with Iris!' she said shrilly. 'Do you understand?'

'You can't stop us,' Calvin said. 'She's working for me as from tomorrow. She's replacing Alice.'

Kit stared at him, her face turning the colour of tallow.

'No!' she said violently. 'I'm not having that! Work for a devil like you? Iris? Oh no, I'll soon stop that!'

'Will you?' Calvin lit a cigarette. 'I don't think so. She wants to work in the bank. How will you stop her? Why shouldn't she work for her future father-in-law?'

'I'm not having her shut up with a swine like you!' Kit said. 'I know what you could do to her with your slimy charm.'

Calvin smiled.

'Oh, come. Don't be ridiculous.' His expression suddenly changed and he glared at her. 'Listen, you drunken fool, can't you see why it is important she should work with me in the bank? I will have the opportunity to hear from her what her boy-friend is up to. Don't make any mistakes about him. He's smart and he could be dangerous. And another thing: it is important to both of us she should work in the bank rather than a stranger. If I had a stranger working for me, I would never know if she might come across the money when I'm not there. It isn't likely anyone will find the money, but I'm not taking any chances. If by some stroke of bad luck, Iris did come across it, I can't imagine she would send her mother to the gas chamber.'

'I'd rather that than expose her to your beastliness,' Kit said, glaring at him. 'She's not working for you! That's final! Now get out!'

Calvin studied her, his face suddenly expressionless. Then with a slight shrug of his powerful shoulders, he got to his feet and returned to his room. He heard the lock of the door snap after him.

He sat down and for some twenty minutes he remained motionless, humming under his breath. Then suddenly he got to his feet, listened intently for some moments, then hearing nothing, he stepped silently into the passage and moved across to the bathroom. He went in and closed the door. He examined the small, flimsy bolt on the door. . . . There was no lock. He fingered the bolt, then taking a penknife from his pocket, he squatted down and loosened the four small screws. He then slid the bolt home and gently tried to open the door. The bolt held, but only just. He knew a quick hard jerk would wrench the bolt off the door.

Satisfied, he returned to his room. Shutting himself in,

he went to the closet and took from it a box of golf balls. Four of these he dropped into an odd sock he took from a drawer. He swung the sock. It made an extremely vicious and efficient cosh.

He sat down to wait. The time was now half past nine. In another hour, Kit would take a bath.

He considered his plan for ridding himself of her. It was safe and simple. She had been drinking. When he heard her in the bath he would wrench off the bolt on the bathroom door, enter, slam her over the head with the improvised cosh, then hold her under the water until she was dead. He would leave her body in the bath for Flo to find. The fact the bolt was so flimsy, it would be assumed that Flo had wrenched it off when opening the door.

It was safe and simple, but he decided he had better have an alibi in case something went wrong. Leaving the cosh on the bed, he went downstairs. The television set was on, and from the sound of the gunfire, Calvin guessed the old couple were enjoying yet another gangster movie. He went to the door of the darkened room.

'Sorry to interrupt,' he said. 'I'll be in the garage. I have car trouble. If there is a telephone call for me, could I bother you to let me know?'

Major Hardy dragged his attention from the lighted screen.

'Certainly, my dear chap,' he said. 'Is there any news yet of Alice?'

'Nothing. I'll let you know as soon as there is,' and Calvin backed out of the room.

He went to the garage, rolled up his sleeves and quickly removed the sparking plugs from the engine. As he worked, he hummed tunelessly under his breath, his fleshy face set. He scraped a little carbon from the plugs, then leaving them on the work bench, he silently returned to the house. He crept up the stairs and entered his room. The time was now close on half past ten. The gangster movie with all its noise and violence would run to eleven. Even if Kit had time to scream, the old couple wouldn't hear her. Calvin sat down, holding the cosh in his hand and waited.

Minutes dragged by. At half past ten, he suddenly wondered if Kit were too drunk to take a bath. She might have fallen asleep. He got to his feet and moved to the communicating door. Putting his ear against the panel of the door, he listened. He heard nothing. He was tempted to see if the door was still locked, but he was afraid of alerting her.

He went back to his chair and sat down. There were other nights, he told himself, but as each day went by, the danger increased.

He lit a cigarette. Faintly, he could hear the television set downstairs. He looked at his watch. Then he heard a sound from the other room that brought him to his feet, tense and listening. A minute or so passed. He could now hear Kit moving around her room. Then he heard her door open and he heard her walk across the passage and into the bathroom. He heard the bathroom door close.

A vicious little grin lit up his face and he opened his door to peer into the passage. The thick fingers of his right hand gripped the cosh. Above the sound from the television, he could hear the bath water running. He stood waiting. After what seemed an eternity, the water ceased to run. He moved into the passage. With cat-like silence, he reached the bathroom door and paused to listen again. He heard the sound of water as if Kit had stepped into the bath. He was breathing lightly and rapidly and he was aware that his heart was beating unsteadily. His lips came off his teeth in a vicious grin as he turned the door handle. When it was as far back as it would go and as yet another burst of gun-fire came from the television set, he gave the door a sudden shove forward. He heard the bolt drop on to the tiled floor as the door jerked open. He moved quickly into the bathroom.

He paused, his right hand, holding the cosh, half swinging up, his heart suddenly skipping a beat.

Kit stood with her back against the far wall, some twelve feet from Calvin. She held a loofa in her left hand which dripped water. Calvin guessed at once that she had been using the loofa to disturb the bath water, leading him to believe she was in the bath.

In her right hand, she held a ·38 automatic, its blunt nose pointing directly at Calvin. She was still wearing her polka-dot nylon wrap and there was a fixed little smile on her white face that sent a sudden chill up Calvin's spine. He had an instinctive feeling that she was about to shoot him.

'Don't be a fool!' he rapped out. 'You'll never touch the money if you shoot!'

They were the right words. The awful little smile slipped from her mouth and her brown, glittering eyes suddenly lost their mad blank stare.

For a long tense moment, they stared at each other. The gun remained pointing at him, but he knew the danger for the moment was over.

Then she said, 'Yes ... I was forgetting. You clever devil! You just saved your beastly life by saying the right thing at absolutely the right moment. You follow a pattern, don't you? You use women and then you get rid of them, but you're not getting rid of me!'

Calvin was eyeing the gun in her hand. The sight of the gun shocked him. His great strength against her feeble strength was useless in the face of the gun. He measured the distance between them. He might just possibly reach her and smash the gun out of her hand, but he was sure he couldn't prevent her firing the gun before he did reach her.

Even above the racket the television was making, the old couple would hear the shot.

'It was a mistake,' he said, keeping the snarl out of his voice with an effort. 'You scare me, Kit, with your drinking. I acted on impulse.'

'Don't act on another impulse,' she said, staring fixedly at him. 'I'll kill you if I have to, so don't do anything stupid.'

'I'm not going to do anything. It's all right.'

'Didn't you think I knew what you were planning?' She went on. 'Couldn't you see how obvious it was to me. I help you get the money, then I go the way Alice went and you have all the money, but that's not how it's going to work out, Dave. I knew sooner or later you would try to murder me. I set a trap for you and you walked into it. I didn't drink your whisky. I poured it down the sink. I'm not such a drunk as you imagine. Then when I saw you had loosened the bolt on the door, I knew you would be in here to murder me. Well, you're not murdering me. You're not as smart as you think you are. And another thing, Iris isn't working for you. You're going to keep your filthy hands off her. Do you understand?'

Calvin switched on his charm.

'Don't let's quarrel, Kit,' he said. 'I've already explained . . .'

'You're in for a surprise,' Kit broke in. 'Up to now you have handled this, but from now on, I'm handling it and you'll do what I tell you.'

'You can't handle it,' Calvin said. 'You're in no condition to handle anything. You're drunk. You've got to face it. You've got to leave this to me.'

Slowly, she lowered the gun.

'You'd be happy if I were dead, wouldn't you, but I'm not going to die. While you were being so clever arranging to steal all that money, I too have been arranging how to protect myself. If I die, Dave, you'll go to the gas chamber. I've fixed it for you.' She put the gun down on top of the toilet seat. 'If you think I am bluffing, go ahead and hit me over the head with your cosh and then drown me. Then see where it gets you.'

Calvin studied her, feeling hot sweat running down his back, aware his heart was thumping and there was a dry, sour taste in his mouth.

They stared at each other for a long moment, then he slowly backed out of the bathroom. Leaving the gun where it was, she followed him. He moved into his bedroom and she came in after him, closing the door.

He had her now. She was defenceless and he could see she was half drunk. He gripped the sock between his thick fingers. A quick movement and she would be lying at his feet. The bath was already filled. All he had to do . . .

But he knew by the mocking way she was staring at him that she had beaten him and with a sudden vicious movement, he threw the sock of golf balls across the room.

She leaned against the door, folding her arms across her breasts and she suddenly laughed: a hard, dry, mirthless sound.

'That's right, Dave. Now you're showing some sense at last. When you were at the bank this morning, I wrote a letter. It was a long, complicated letter and it took me nearly all the morning. In it I set down everything you and I have done, how you murdered Alice and where you have hidden the money. There isn't one thing we haven't done together I haven't written down. I've taken this letter to an attorney – never mind who – and I have told him to read the letter and act on it when I am dead. So long as I remain alive, Dave, you'll remain alive, but if you try any of your bright murderous ideas, then you'll follow me to the grave.'

Calvin ran his thick fingers through his hair. He

moved away from her, rage burning inside him.

'So now we'll get married,' Kit went on, 'and we'll go away as we planned. Then you'll give me my share of the money. But from now on, Dave, you're going to do what I tell you . . . do you understand?'

In the long pause as they looked at each other, they both heard the telephone bell ringing. Calvin went out into the passage. His legs felt unsteady and there was a feeling of fear and rage constricting his heart.

Major Hardy called up to him from the hall.

'It's the police, Mr. Calvin,' he said. 'They want to speak to you.'

Calvin hurried down and picked up the telephone receiver.

It was Easton to tell him they had found Alice's body.

CHAPTER THREE

I

CALVIN sat at the wheel of his car, his eyes staring into the lane of light made by the car's headlights, his mind busy.

Sheriff Thomson had said over the telephone that he would be glad if Calvin would come down to his office right away. There was to be an emergency meeting and they would be glad of his help.

The time was now a few minutes to eleven. There was scarcely any traffic on the road. A few spots of rain showed on the windshield.

Calvin was thinking of Kit. The situation was dangerous unless she had been bluffing, but he had an uneasy feeling she hadn't been. She had now put herself beyond his reach, but that was not all. She could walk in front of a car, fall ill, meet her death in dozens of accidental ways and this damned attorney would then open her letter and Calvin would be sunk. He must think of some way to persuade her to get the letter back from the attorney. It was intolerable to know that his life depended on her own span of life.

He suddenly became aware of a red light flashing in the middle of the road and he hastily braked, bringing the car to a stop in front of a police car that half blocked the road.

Two police officers approached him. He saw beyond them, two other policemen, guns in hands.

He leaned out of the car window, his mouth turning dry. One police officer turned the beam of a flashlight on him.

'Identify yourself, please,' he said curtly.

Calvin took out his wallet and handed it over.

'What's all this in aid of?' he asked, forcing his voice to sound casual.

'Why, it's Mr. Calvin,' the police officer said and suddenly grinned. 'We're looking for your bank robber. Every car in and out of Pittsville is being checked.'

Calvin said, startled, 'But he left town forty-eight hours ago, didn't he?'

'Someone thinks he didn't,' the police officer said, returning Calvin's wallet. He stepped back and saluted. 'Okay, Mr. Calvin, go right on ahead.'

Calvin drove on. There was a set expression on his fleshy face and his eyes were uneasy. Why did they think the man they were after hadn't left town? he wondered. Had he made a slip somewhere?

He was in for another little jolt as he pulled up outside the sheriff's office. He saw a big red and black Cadillac with San Francisco number plates standing in the parking lot. He knew the car well. It belonged to Henry Marthy, the general manager of the Federal & National Banking Corporation and his boss. What was he doing here at this hour? Drawing in a deep breath, Calvin walked up the flight of steps and entered the sheriff's office.

Marthy was talking to the sheriff. Travers was sitting at a desk, talking on the telephone. As Calvin entered the big room, he heard Travers say, 'A standard Remington: 1959 model? Yeah, fine. Any special characteristics? The letters r and v? Right. Thanks a lot,' and he hung up.

Only half listening, Calvin crossed the room and shook hands with Marthy.

'It's good to see you here, sir,' he said with his charming

smile. 'This is a terrible thing. I'm glad of your support.'

'It certainly is,' Marthy said gravely. 'You heard Miss Craig has been murdered?'

'The sheriff telephoned me,' Calvin said and turning to the sheriff, he went on, 'I didn't get all the details. Where did you find her, sheriff?'

'We found the get-away car in the Downside railroad parking lot. She was in the boot,' the sheriff said. He looked at his massive gold watch. 'Easton will be here any moment now. He should have information for us. Let's sit down.'

As they moved to the big table and began pulling out chairs, the door jerked open and Easton came in. He looked hot and anxious. His fat, weak face glistened with sweat and he wiped his hand on the seat of his trousers before shaking hands with Marthy.

'Let's sit down, gentlemen,' he said. 'I guess you want to know what's been happening.' He waited until Marthy was seated before sitting down himself. Calvin sat opposite Marthy with Travers at the bottom of the table and the sheriff on the other side of Marthy.

'Well, there's no doubt the girl was murdered,' Easton said. 'She was strangled. The M.O. puts the time of her death around two o'clock on the night of the robbery. The way I see it is this: this guy Acres persuaded the girl to help him grab the payroll. He took his time about it. We know he and she were meeting pretty regularly during the past three weeks. Finally, he persuaded her to help him. He sent her a note the day before the robbery reminding her to leave the back entrance to the bank unlocked. Then after the payroll was delivered, and after Mr. Calvin and Alice had left, he walked in, took all the light bulbs out of their sockets, cutting off the alarm system, and unlocked the safe, using Alice's key and a duplicate she had got for him from Calvin's key.'

'Just a moment,' Marthy said sharply. 'Explain that. I

don't understand. How could they have got hold of Calvin's key?'

'When Lamb had his stroke, Miss Craig had the two keys for some hours. That's when we think she took an impression of Calvin's key she later gave to Acres.'

'But Lamb had his stroke more than six weeks ago,' Marthy pointed out. 'Do you mean Acres was hanging around her for six weeks?'

Calvin sat very still, his face expressionless. Easton shifted uneasily.

'I guess so ... he must have done,' he said finally. 'I'm not saying he was hanging around here, but he was in touch with Alice ... how else could he have got at the second key? Calvin tells me once he had possession of the key, it was never out of his sight.'

'That's not exactly correct,' Calvin said a little too quickly. 'I guess Alice could have got at it pretty well any time after Lamb's death. Naturally, I trusted her. I kept my key in my pocket. In hot weather, I left my jacket in the office when I worked in the vault. I guess she could have sneaked into my office and taken an impression of the key.'

Marthy turned and looked hard at Calvin.

'But if you were working in the vault, you would surely need the key to open the vault, wouldn't you?'

Calvin rubbed the side of his jaw, his brain racing. Somehow he managed to keep his face expressionless.

What are you saying, you fool? he thought. Watch it! Another slip like that and you'll be in trouble.

'When the payroll isn't in the vault, sir,' he said, 'we leave the vault door unlocked.'

There was a pause, then Marthy said, 'Well, go on,' this to Easton.

Calvin reached for his pack of cigarettes. He lit a cigarette and drew down a lungful of smoke.

'Acres had arranged to meet Alice after he had the money,' Easton went on. 'She imagined they were going away together, but Acres had other ideas. As soon as he had established the fact they were going to 'Frisco by talking to the gas attendant, he drove her to some lonely spot and strangled her. He dumped her in the boot of the car, ditched the car at the railroad station and then disappeared with the payroll. It now seems pretty certain he is still in the district.'

Calvin leaned back in his chair. His bulk made the chair creak.

Marthy asked in his dry precise voice, 'What makes you think that?'

Easton felt a slight stabbing pain in his stomach. He winced, shifting in his chair.

'We're slowly building up evidence that Acres is a local man. We've had some luck. There's an asylum for the criminal insane at Downside. On the night of the robbery one of the inmates escaped in a stolen car. He got away around the time Acres was driving to Downside after the robbery. The police were alerted and all roads out of Pittsville and Downside were immediately blocked. We know no one left Downside without being checked. The road blocks were so efficient, the nut was captured within half an hour. It so happened that at that time few cars were on the roads and those people checked were known to the police: they were local people. There were no strangers. We are pretty sure Acres didn't get through so he must either be holed up in Downside or in Pittsville.'

Calvin's mouth turned dry. He stared at the glowing end of his cigarette, aware his heart was now thumping so violently he was scared that Travers, sitting close to him, would hear it.

'What makes you think he is a local man?' Marthy asked.

It was Travers who said, 'We think he could be a local man for a number of reasons. The main reason is that Downside and Pittsville are small towns and strangers get noticed. We have been hammering away on the radio and TV all day and half the night giving out with Acre's description. No one has come forward to say they've been sheltering him or even have seen him with the exception of the man who sold him the car and the gas attendant. None of the hotels nor the rooming-houses have had strangers with them. The people at the hotels have all been regulars. We think the black sideboards and the moustache were a disguise. All Acres had to do was to put them on and he became Acres as seen by Mrs. Loring, Major Hardy and Miss Pearson, then take them off to become X, a citizen either of Downside or Pittsville. We know the letter he wrote to Alice was written on a standard Remington typewriter. This means he couldn't have carried the machine around with him. He either borrowed the machine which we think is unlikely or owns the machine which is more likely. The final point is he bought a car in Downside. If he had been an outsider, why should he risk buying a car locally?'

Calvin looked down at his hands. The fine sandy hairs were glistening with sweat in the hard lamplight. He had used the typewriter at the bank to write that letter. He remembered as he had entered the room, Travers asking if the typewriter had any special characteristics. He remembered Travers saying something about the letters r and v.

'Right now,' Travers was saying, 'we are checking where every Remington in Pittsville and Downside is located. We have lists from the local dealers. Then we'll have to check every machine. This is going to take time, but when we find the machine, we'll be pretty close to Mr. Acres.'

'So you think this man is still here and the money also?' Marthy asked.

'That's what we think,' Sheriff Thomson said. 'We've got him in a trap and we're taking good care he doesn't get out of it. The road blocks are going to remain in position and every car will be checked. We have men at the railroad station who'll check every piece of luggage as it leaves. We have men at the mail-sorting office who will check every parcel leaving. It's a big job, but it's being done. As I see it there is no way for him to get the money out. Sooner or later, we'll catch up with him, but it's going to take time.'

'I have a pretty good incentive for you all to work on this job,' Marthy said. 'My directors have decided to offer a reward for this man's arrest. This is the usual bank procedure, but since one of our own staff is involved, we are offering a much higher reward. Anyone, and that includes members of the police, who gives information that will lead to the arrest and conviction of this man will receive the bank reward of sixty thousand dollars. I would be glad if you would arrange to circulate this information as widely as possible.'

Travers stiffened. He drew in a long, deep breath. He was aware of Easton's reaction. Easton was staring at Marthy as if he couldn't believe his ears. Both men were thinking: sixty thousand dollars! Both men were thinking what they could do with the money. Easton was thinking he could afford to get a divorce and marry Mavis Hart. He could retire and buy a little cottage somewhere. Mavis would look after him in his old age.

Travers was thinking, here at last was the chance he had often dreamed about of laying his hands on a large slice of money to provide Iris with a decent home, to get out of Pittsville and buy a partnership in that mink farm Max was always writing to him about.

As Travers sat there, his mind alive with the prospects of winning such a reward, he suddenly became aware that Calvin, sitting close to him, was humming tunelessly under his breath.

2

Ten minutes after the last performance, Iris left the darkened movie house and started the short walk to the bus stop. It was now raining heavily and she walked with her head bent against the driving rain.

A familiar voice called, 'Hey! Iris!'

She looked up and saw Ken Travers leaning out of his car window, waving to her. As she ran towards him, he opened the off-side door.

'Why, Ken,' she said as she scrambled in, 'what are you doing here? What a surprise!'

They kissed. She was immediately aware how tense he was and she drew away to look sharply at him.

'Is there something wrong? It's not Kit . . .?'

'Nothing's wrong,' he said and put his arm around her, holding her against him. 'I had to see you, honey. I've taken time off and came over. The sheriff and Easton are holding the fort, but I've got to get back within an hour.' He looked at her, his face alight with excitement. 'Something's come up that could affect us both . . . something pretty good.'

'What is it? Something's come up with me, too, that's pretty good. I'm so glad you came. I wanted to talk to you about it.'

'What is it?'

'No, you tell me first.'

'The bank is offering a reward for the bank robber,' Ken said. 'Sixty thousand dollars! Can you imagine!

Sixty thousand dollars and I'm pretty sure I'm going to get it!'

Iris gasped.

'Oh, Ken. You really think you'll get it?'

'I guess so.' Travers tightened his grip on her. 'If I got all that money, your mother wouldn't object to us marrying would she? I mean the only thing she had against me is that I'm not earning enough. That's the only thing, isn't it?'

'She has nothing against you,' Iris said. 'It's just that she has had such a rough time, she doesn't want me to live the way she did. Yes, of course, if we had all that money, Kit would be wild with joy. I'm sure she would!'

'That's what I hoped you would say,' Travers said, staring through the rain-drenched windshield. 'You remember Max Heldon? The guy I went to school with and who started that mink farm out at Westfields? You remember I told you he wanted me to go in as partner, but I hadn't the money? Well, he wrote to me last week. He's doing fine, but he still wants a partner: someone who will put up twenty thousand dollars for expansion. How would it be if we went out there and worked with him on the farm? With the forty thousand we'd have over, we could build a pretty nice house and furnish it the way we want and still have something over. How would you like that . . . bringing up baby mink?'

Iris closed her eyes, then opening them, she sighed with ecstasy.

'I'd love it! But what makes you think you can get the reward? I mean . . . there's the sheriff and Easton . . . wouldn't they want to share it with you?'

'The terms are that anyone giving information that will lead to the arrest and conviction of the murderer gets the reward,' Travers said. 'I'm practically certain I know who killed Alice although I have still to get the proof. Neither

Easton nor the sheriff are on to him, and that gives me more than a head start. If I work fast and get the proof, then I'm entitled to the reward.'

'You know who did it?' Iris said, staring at him. 'You mean you know where this man Acres is hiding?'

'Acres doesn't exist. He never has existed,' Travers said quietly. 'He is a dummy figure in sideboards and a moustache. After he showed himself to a few people, got the money and murdered Alice, he took off the sideboards and the moustache and returned to his apparently respectable self.'

'You mean it is someone living in Pittsville.'

'Either Pittsville or Downside.'

'You know who he is?'

'I'm pretty sure, although I can't actually prove it, but I will.'

'Who is he? Anyone I know?'

Travers hesitated.

'This is going to be a shock to you, honey. It'll take a bit of believing, but I'm sure I'm right.' He paused, then went on, 'It's Calvin.'

Iris stared incredulously at him.

'Mr. Calvin? You think he killed Alice? Why, Ken, what are you saying? How can you possibly say such a thing?'

'I know it's pretty hard to take,' Travers said, 'but when you know all the facts and put two and two together, it's the only possible solution to the mysterious Johnny Acres.'

'But, Ken! You can't say things like this! Kit's in love with him . . . they are getting married! How can you!'

'I haven't forgotten your mother. That's one of the reasons why I've come here tonight to talk it over with you. She wouldn't want to be trapped into marrying a killer, would she? Isn't it better for her to know now than when it's too late?'

'I don't believe it! You're just guessing. You said you haven't any proof!'

'I know . . . I haven't yet. I only realized it was Calvin about an hour ago. But I'll get proof. I'm sure of that. Look, let me tell you just why I'm so sure it is Calvin.'

'I don't want to hear!' Iris said, white and tense. 'I'm sure you're wrong . . .'

'How can you be sure unless you hear what I've got to tell you?' Travers said patiently. 'Now, listen, for more than five years, week after week, the payroll has been delivered to the bank and has been safe. Then Calvin becomes manager: six weeks later the payroll vanishes.'

'But that doesn't mean anything! It could have vanished when Mr. Lamb was there!'

'It could have, but it didn't. I'm pretty sure Calvin made up his mind to steal the payroll almost as soon as he got here. He knew if the payroll vanished only two people would be suspected . . . himself or Alice. It had to be an inside job. No outsider would know how to put the alarm system out of order nor get at the keys to the vault. He was smart enough to know this so he decided to pin the blame on Alice. During the first three weeks he was at the bank, he worked on Alice. He has a way with women. You have only to look at him to realize it. No man has ever bothered to look at Alice, now Calvin turns on all his charm, and after a while she falls for him hook, line and sinker.'

'You're wrong!' Iris said, thumping her clenched fists on her knees. 'I know you're wrong! Alice wouldn't . . .'

'I know . . . I know . . . I said just that when Easton said he thought Alice had fallen for Acres. I could see that couldn't jell, but Calvin had eight hours a day for three weeks to work on her more or less alone. Of course, in that time, he could do it . . . and he did it!'

Iris hesitated, realizing what Travers had said made sense, then thinking of Kit, she said, 'I don't believe it!'

'All right, but let me finish. Assuming I'm right and Alice really fell for him, the rest was pretty easy. By then he had announced his engagement to your mother. Now he tells Alice he has made a mistake. It is she he loves and not your mother, but the engagement is official. He has to be careful. He doesn't want to get landed with a breach of promise suit. That's the sort of blah Alice could have fallen for. She would have been flattered he preferred her to your mother. She would want to protect his reputation as a banker. Then he puts up the idea of grabbing the payroll and both of them vanishing. I'm not saying it didn't take him a lot of careful work and persuasion, but finally he got her to agree to help him. So they could go out together without gossip, I reckon he disguised himself as Johnny Acres ... anyway, that was his story to Alice and being a romantic little dope, she fell for that too. She imagined he really loved her and was taking all this trouble to disguise himself so he could steal a few hours out of working hours with her. She probably got a kick out of sneaking out of the house to meet him when she was supposed to be working for her exam, but all the time Calvin was establishing Acres, planning to pin the robbery on her, and finally planning to murder her when he got the money.'

'Stop!' Iris cried, facing him. 'You know as well as I do this is malicious nonsense! You can't prove one word of all this! Ken! What's come over you? How can you say such things?'

'Oh, I agree it sounds far-fetched,' Travers said, 'but let's look at this mysterious Johnny Acres. Only a very few people – five to be exact – have seen him. No one has come forward to say he stayed with them during the three weeks he is supposed to have been courting Alice. Where did he stay? If he is Calvin, we know where he stayed, but if he isn't Calvin, where did he hide himself? He is tall and heavily built. So is Calvin. He wore sideboards and a moustache. Calvin is clean shaven, but it is easy to stick crepe hair on your face.' Seeing Iris was about to interrupt him, he raised his hand. 'Now wait . . . here's the clincher that set me off. The car salesman who sold Acres the getaway car said Acres had an irritating habit of humming under his breath . . . those were his words. This seems to be an unconscious habit. The man probably doesn't know he does it. Well, Calvin has exactly the same habit . . . he too hums tunelessly under his breath. What do you say now?'

Iris started to say something, then stopped.

'Now look,' Travers said, 'I have no real proof, but I have a lead, and Easton and the sheriff so far haven't this lead. I'm thinking of you and me and the reward. This man Acres typed a letter to Alice. It was typed on a standard Remington with two defective letters: the r and the v are slightly out of alignment. I want to find out if the bank has such a machine. It's my guess it has. If it has, I then want to find out if Calvin ever owned a fawn, belted overcoat. If he has owned one, then I guess I've got enough on him to make an arrest. Then there is the payroll. Where is it? He must have hidden it somewhere. He can't have moved it out of town. He's forced to sit on it . . . but where?'

'I still don't believe a word of this,' Iris said, but Travers could see she was shaken. 'You may as well know, Ken: I'm taking Alice's place. I'm starting work tomorrow.'

Travers twisted around in his seat to stare at her.

'Oh no, you're not! You're not working for Calvin! You're not . . .' He stopped short, seeing the angry flush rise to her face. Controlling his voice, he went on, 'What about Dix? You leaving him?'

'Yes . . . Mr. Calvin asked me to help him. The money's better and I'm going to.'

'But after what I've told you, honey, you wouldn't want to work for him, would you?'

'Let's go home. Nothing you have said so far has convinced me that you're right. I'm going to work for Dave Calvin and that's the end of it.'

Travers's mind worked fast. He knew Iris well enough to realize that the more pressure he put on her the more obstinate she would become.

'All right, then work for him if you must, but when you walk into the bank tomorrow morning, look at the typewriter. If it is a standard Remington, you'll know what I've been saying isn't so cockeyed. You'll probably be using the machine, see if the letters r and v are out of alignment. That's all I ask. Check the typewriter and if it isn't a Remington, I'll admit I'm way off the beam.'

'All right,' Iris said. 'I'll do it, but I'm quite sure even if it is a Remington, Dave Calvin has nothing to do with this robbery.'

Travers shrugged his shoulders. He drove the car fast to the highway. He was a little deflated, but still convinced he was right. Neither of them said anything until Travers pulled up outside the rooming-house. The time was now half past one.

'Good night, Ken,' Iris said stiffly as she made to get out of the car.

Travers slipped his arm around her and pulled her to him.

'Don't let's quarrel, honey,' he said. 'I may be wrong, but if I'm not, it's going to be all right between us, isn't it?'

'I'm thinking of Kit,' Iris said. 'Oh, Ken, even if you are right . . . I do hope you're not! I wouldn't want that money, knowing how unhappy Kit would be . . . but I'm sure you're wrong.'

Travers kissed her. Breaking away, Iris got out of the car and ran up the drive towards the house.

She paused at the front door, listening to Travers driving

away, then she unlocked the door and entered the dark hall. She went silently up to her bedroom. She was surprised to see a light coming from under her door. Turning the handle, she walked in.

Kit was sitting in an armchair, smoking. Her face was pale and her brown eyes were unnaturally bright. Iris paused in the doorway to stare at her.

'Why, Kit! Why aren't you in bed?'

'I wanted to talk to you,' Kit said. 'Come in and shut the door.'

Iris shut the door and went over to sit on the bed.

'Dave tells me you are going to work at the bank,' Kit said. 'Why didn't you tell me?'

Her cold, hostile voice startled Iris.

'You weren't there when he asked me. I – I thought he had told you,' Iris said. 'Why? You don't mind, do you?'

'Yes, I mind. You're only a kid. I don't want you to be exposed to Dave's charm.'

Iris felt her face grow hot.

'I don't know what you mean.'

'Don't you?' Kit's bleak eyes frightened her. 'I think you do. I'm going to marry him. I'm twice your age. I'm not anything like as pretty as you. The less you see of him, the better it will be for me.'

'Kit!' Iris jumped to her feet. 'You don't know what you're saying!'

'You mean I'm drunk?' Kit smiled bitterly. 'I guess I am.' She passed her hand across her eyes. 'You're not going to work for Dave. Do you understand? I forbid it.'

There was a long pause, then Iris said quietly and steadily, 'I'm sorry, but I am. It's all arranged. It's a good job and I need the money. I'm sure you don't know what you are saying. Please go to bed.'

Kit remained motionless. Her head throbbed. Her brain felt as if it were in a covering of cotton-wool. She wished now she hadn't had that last drink.

'Kit . . . it's late. Please go to bed,' Iris said.

Unsteadily, Kit got to her feet.

'All right, you poor little fool,' she said, her words slurred, 'then work for him if you want to, but don't say I didn't warn you. I don't care . . . I don't care a damn what happens to him or to you or to me,' and lurching a little, she went out of the room.

Iris listened to her mother's stumbling steps as she climbed the stairs. She felt a cold chill crawl up her spine, and involuntarily, she shivered.

CHAPTER FOUR

I

A LITTLE after six o'clock the following morning, Kit woke with a start. She became aware that someone was tapping softly and persistently on her door.

She half sat up. Her head felt heavy and her eyes burned. She looked towards the bedside clock as she called, 'Who is it?'

'Dave! Open up! I've got to talk to you.' Calvin's voice was pitched low. There was a note of urgency in it that alerted her.

She threw off the bedclothes, snatched up a wrap and struggled into it as she crossed the room and unlocked the door.

Calvin, his face set, a cold, bleak expression in his eyes, came in and shut the door.

'What is it?' she demanded, moving away from him. She picked up a comb from the dressing-table and ran it through her hair. 'What is it?'

'I tried to get you last night,' he snarled, 'but you were so drunk you didn't hear me knocking.'

'What is it?' she repeated. She stared at herself in the mirror, seeing the shadows under her eyes and the gaunt tightness of her skin. She grimaced and looked away.

'Trouble.' He paused, then went on, 'Have you a type-writer?'

She stared at him, startled. Her head was beginning to ache.

'A typewriter? Yes . . . why?'

'Where is it?'

She motioned to where a battered portable stood against the wall. He picked it up, rested it on the bed and lifted the lid. It was an old Smith Corona.

'Does it work?'

'Yes . . . what is all this?'

'I wrote that damned letter to Alice on the bank's type-writer. The police have found out it was written on a standard Remington with faulty letters. If they find the machine, we're in a hell of a jam.'

She stiffened, her eyes growing large.

'You and your fool-proof plan!' she said, her voice going shrill. 'Now what are you going to do?'

'Keep your voice down! I'll get rid of the Remington and use this.' He nodded to the portable. 'If they ask, I'll tell them I found the machine in the bank. Lamb's dying and can't be questioned. Alice can't answer questions either.'

'How will you get rid of the Remington?'

'I'll hide it in the vault.'

She relaxed a little.

'Then take the portable and get out!'

'I haven't finished yet. That letter you've sent to your attorney. You've got to get it back. You don't seem to realize if anything happens to you, the spot I'll be in,' Calvin said, trying to make his voice sound casual. 'At the rate you're drinking, you could drop dead any time, then where would I be?'

She smiled jeeringly at him.

'You tried to murder me last night . . . remember? Why should I care what happens to you? Get out!'

'I want that letter!'

'You're not getting it!'

They stared at each other, their hate white hot, then Calvin, realizing there was nothing he could do to force her to give him the letter, suddenly shrugged. He would have to bring pressure on her somehow, but now wasn't the time to worry about that. He had more vital things to cope with.

'You know Iris is working for me?' he said. 'You were so drunk last night I don't know if you remember.'

'I remember,' Kit said, looking at him strangely. 'I tried to stop her, but I couldn't. I'm warning you. If you try any of your tricks with her, I'll kill you. I'm not warning you again.'

The cold baleful expression in her eyes made him uneasy. He remembered the gun.

'Where did you get the gun from?' he asked, watching her.

'It was my husband's,' she said. 'He taught me how to use it. I'm a good shot, Dave . . . remember that.'

He dismissed this with an impatient wave of his hand.

'Give me the gun. In your condition, you're not safe to own a gun. Come on . . . give it to me.'

She sneered at him.

'It's where you'll never find it. Get out!'

'I must have been crazy to have picked on you,' he said, having to control the urge to take her by the throat and strangle her.

'Think so?' She laughed. 'Well, you're stuck with me. When are we getting married? What a couple we'll make! I want to get out of this hole and start spending some money!'

'You'll be lucky if you ever touch the money. They have this town sewn up tight. They're even checking every parcel and every piece of luggage leaving town. We now may have to wait a damn sight longer than I thought before either of us touches it!'

'I want some money now!' Kit said, leaning forward and glaring at him. 'I haven't enough to last until the end of the week! I want that three hundred I lent you.'

'Where do you imagine it's coming from? It went towards buying the car.'

'Then get it from the bank! I must have it! Take it from the payroll!'

'Stop drinking and you'll have enough,' Calvin said and snatching up the portable typewriter, he went back into his room.

He stood looking out of the window for some minutes. He had passed a bad night. He felt limp and his head was heavy. This wasn't working out the way he had planned, but he was thankful he had been called to the emergency meeting. If he hadn't known about the typewriter he could have been in a hell of a spot. He rested his hot forehead against the glass of the window. He would have to be careful no one saw him take the portable into the bank. He would have to watch every move now that he made. One slip and they would be on to him.

He turned away from the window, opened his closet and took out his hold-all. He put the portable in the bag. On top of it, he put one of his suits. He looked at his watch. The time was ten minutes to seven. He would have to get to the bank before anyone arrived so he could take the Remington down into the vault. He would conceal it in yet another of the deed boxes.

Picking up the hold-all, he went down to the kitchen. He made himself a cup of coffee and carried it into the living-room. The house was strangely quiet. He sat down, drank the coffee and lit a cigarette. He considered his future plans. There was danger, of course. The Johnny Acres impersonation hadn't been such a hot idea after all. Would they finally come around to suspecting that he had impersonated Acres? It would be a long shot. He thought it unlikely. But the fact they now thought Acres was a local man made him very uneasy. It might be necessary to lay a red herring for them, taking their suspicions away from him ... but how? He thought of Iris sleeping upstairs. He might use her. It was an idea he filed away in his mind. This bank reward made his situation even more dangerous. He had seen Travers's change of expression when Marthy had announced the reward. Calvin was pretty sure what had been going through Travers's mind. With sixty thousand dollars, Travers would cease to be small-time: he could marry Iris: he could take her away from Pittsville. Calvin was suddenly thankful he had picked on Kit to help him. If Travers became dangerous, he would use Kit to protect himself. Travers wouldn't send his future mother-in-law to the gas chamber. The sheriff and Easton were has-beens. If it came to a show-down, he could muzzle Travers. Thinking about it, Calvin gained confidence. He would have to be careful, but if things went wrong, he could put the screws on Travers.

He arrived at the bank a few minutes after eight o'clock. He parked his car, then carrying the hold-all, he walked up the main street towards the bank.

As he reached the short path leading to the bank entrance, he saw Travers come out of the sheriff's office and walk rapidly towards him. Calvin paused. He felt very confident. This tall, rangy young fellow might be smart, but Calvin was now sure he had him where he wanted him. He walked towards him. The two men met half-way between the sheriff's office and the bank.

'Hello there,' Calvin said smiling. 'Any news? Anything happening?'

Travers shook his head, his eyes going to the hold-all.

'Nothing right now. You're early.' He paused, then went on, 'Are you going away?'

Calvin laughed easily.

'No such luck. I'm taking a suit to be cleaned. Yes . . . I'm early. We're doing an audit. For the next day or so, I'll have to work for my living.' He looked steadily at Travers. 'Iris has volunteered to help out. Did she tell you? She's taking Alice's place.'

Travers nodded.

'Yes . . . she told me,' he said curtly.

There was a pause. Both men stared intently at each other.

'She'll be a great help,' Calvin said, paused, then went on, scarcely concealing a sneer. 'Wish you luck with that reward. Sixty thousand! It's money! Don't let Easton beat you to it.'

'I won't,' Travers said, his voice quiet. 'I mean to get it.'

'Well, good luck,' and switching on his charming smile, Calvin turned away and began to walk back to the bank, aware that Travers was staring after him.

Suddenly Travers said, 'Hey! One minute!'

Calvin felt a prickle of apprehension crawl up his spine. He turned and waited.

Travers came up in five long, swinging strides.

'I forgot to ask you . . . what kind of typewriter do you use in the bank?'

Calvin lifted his sand-coloured eyebrows. The effort he had to make to keep his face expressionless quickened his heartbeat.

'Typewriter? Typewriter?' he said vaguely, then his smile widened. 'Of course . . . I see. You're looking for a standard Remington with defective letters. No luck, I'm afraid. We use a Smith Corona portable. Don't ask me why. It was here when I came.'

'A portable?' Travers said, staring at him. 'That's unusual, isn't it?'

'My dear fella, who am I to question the meanness of banks?' Calvin said. 'Ours isn't a very important branch, you know. We don't have many letters to write.' He met Travers's searching stare. 'Anything else you'd like to know?'

'No ... thanks.'

'Then I'll get along,' and nodding, Calvin turned and walked towards the bank.

He unlocked the door, entered and relocked the door.

Phew! he thought. That was close ... too close!

He set down the hold-all and walked quickly behind the counter to where the Remington typewriter stood. He picked it up and carried it down to the vault. It took him over a quarter of an hour to find a deed box that contained only a few papers. Into this deed box, he put the typewriter. He went up the stairs and took the portable out of its case. He set the machine on the felt mat where the Remington had stood.

He then emptied the mail box and taking the mail into his office, he began to work.

A few minutes to nine o'clock, Iris arrived. As Calvin opened the door and let her in, she gave him an uncertain smile.

She had slept badly. Although she had tried to put out of her mind Ken's insinuations, the more she thought about what he had said as she had tossed and turned in the darkness, the more she realized that he had something of a case against Calvin.

'You're early,' she said, trying to sound casual. 'Flo told me you had already begun work. Why didn't you call me?'

'It's my hard luck I had to start early ... not yours. The auditors will be here in a few minutes. Come and help me with the mail.'

As she followed him into his office, she saw the portable typewriter standing on the counter. Involuntarily, she stopped short to stare at it. Calvin paused, watching her. He saw her stiffen as she continued to stare at the typewriter. He became instantly alert. What's going on in her mind? he asked himself. Has Travers told her about the Remington? Has he told her to spy on me? Does he suspect that I am Acres? He could do. Why did he ask me what typewriter we use here if he wasn't suspicious?

He said, 'Not much of a machine, is it? It's the best I can do for you. I've already asked the powers-that-be for something better, but so far it hasn't been forthcoming.'

Iris dragged her eyes away from the typewriter. She forced herself to remain calm. She could see the portable didn't fit the felt mat which was obviously designed for a much larger machine.

'Oh, I'll manage,' she said. 'I like the touch of a portable. Kit has one. I often use it.'

'You do? Then you'll be happy with this one. Well, come on: let's see what's in the mail.'

Iris resisted the impulse to go to the machine and examine it. It looked vaguely familiar, but she was aware that Calvin was watching her. His blue eyes were as expressionless and as hard as glass.

They entered the office as a rap came on the bank door.

'There are the auditors,' Calvin said. 'I'll let them in.'

The two auditors entered, exchanged greetings with Calvin and nodded to Iris.

For the next hour, Iris was kept busy discovering banking procedure which Calvin explained to her with a patience that surprised her.

A little after ten o'clock, the first customer came in and Calvin went to serve him.

Left on her own, Iris crossed over to the portable typewriter. She had the excuse to use the machine as Calvin, during the past hour, had dictated several letters. She sat on the high stool, uneasily aware that only some forty hours ago, Alice had also sat on this stool. She looked at the machine and a sudden chill ran through her.

This was Kit's typewriter! She recognized it at once. There was a deep scratch on the metal casing and two of the keys had turned slightly yellow. It was unmistakable.

Her mind confused, her heart thumping, she somehow managed to type the letter. Her eyes kept going to the large felt mat on which the typewriter was standing. She could see the deep impression of the feet of another and bigger machine embedded in the felt.

It wasn't until close on twelve o'clock, that Calvin had the chance to speak to her alone. He had been continuously busy with various customers and the auditors. Now, he came over to her to take the letters she had ready for him.

'How are you getting along?' he asked. 'Are you liking the job?'

'Yes ... of course.' Iris tried to meet the staring blue eyes, but couldn't. To cover her confusion, she slid off the stool and moved away from him.

I've got to watch her, Calvin thought. She's turning hostile. She must have recognized the machine. Damn it! I should have thought of that. If Travers has set her to spy on me, this could be dangerous.

'Are you going home to lunch?' he asked as the two auditors left the bank. 'I usually go across the road. It's not bad. Care to join me?'

'I'll go home,' Iris said quickly. 'Thanks all the same. It'll only take me ten minutes on the bus.'

'Please yourself. I'll lock up. You get off.'

Iris went into the washroom and put on her coat. On the glass shelf above the toilet basin was a box of tissues and a tube of face cream that had belonged to Alice. She looked at these two symbols that represented a memory of the dead girl and she shivered. Hurriedly, she left the washroom, anxious to leave the bank and not remain alone with Calvin. The bank door was already locked. Calvin was standing in his office doorway, waiting. Iris felt a cold, restricting pressure around her heart as the blue, uncanny eyes moved over her.

She paused, and they looked at each other, then Calvin switched on his charm, but for the first time, Iris felt afraid of him.

'If you would like to borrow my car to get home, do use it,' Calvin said.

'I – I won't, thank you. I don't like driving other people's cars.' She moved to the door. Not waiting for him to unlock the door, she turned the key, jerked open the door and walked quickly down the path.

Calvin watched her go. His fleshy face set into a snarling mask.

Iris felt a surge of relief run through her as she saw Ken Travers come out of the sheriff's office and start towards her. She had to restrain herself from breaking into a run. During the brief interval before they came face to face, she had regained her composure.

'Why, Ken . . . you're always turning up,' she said, smiling at him. 'Don't say you have a free hour?'

He slid his arm around her and unmindful of the people passing, he kissed her.

'I've been waiting for you, honey,' he said. 'The old man says it's okay for me to buy you lunch.'

'Why, that's wonderful! I was going home.'

'Let's go across the road. The food there isn't so lousy.'

Remembering that Calvin had said he lunched at this restaurant, Iris said sharply, 'No . . . let's go some place else. Anywhere, but there.'

Travers looked at her, his eyebrows lifting. He could see she was upset about something, and slipping his arm through hers, he steered her towards his car.

'Okay: there's a joint I know . . . it's not bad: not as good as this one, but it'll do.'

They said nothing until they reached the car and got in, then as Travers started the engine, Iris said, breathlessly, 'I'm sorry, Ken, about last night. I now think you are right about Calvin.'

Travers looked sharply at her.

'What's happened to make you change your mind?'

Iris told him about the portable typewriter.

'It belongs to Kit,' she concluded. 'I used it only the other day. It is standing on a mat much too large for it. You can see the impression on the mat of a standard machine.'

Travers was very alert now. He remembered the hold-all Calvin had been carrying.

'Now, at last, we're getting somewhere! I asked him this morning what machine the bank used. He said the Smith Corona portable was at the bank when he came. We've caught him out in his first lie! He knew about the machine because he was at the meeting last night and we tipped him off! The Remington must still be in the bank. He hasn't had a chance of getting rid of it. Any idea where he could have hidden it?'

Iris, pale and as excited as Travers, thought for a moment.

'There's not many places. There's a cupboard in his office. There's the men's room and the vault.'

'What chances have you of finding it?'

'I don't know. He's not likely to leave me alone in the bank. He keeps the keys to the vault. I haven't any right to go into his office while he's not in it. Couldn't you get a search warrant?'

'I could, but if I did I would be tipping my hand to

Easton. He's just as anxious as I am to get the reward. I've got to get a better case against Calvin before I do tip my hand.' He thought for a moment. 'Look, there must be hundreds of carbon copies of letters typed on this Remington in the files. Could you get me one of those carbons ... anyone will do? I'll be able to check from the carbon if it is the Remington we are looking for. With that as proof, I could get a search warrant.'

Iris drew in a deep breath.

'I keep thinking of Kit ...'

'I know, but it's better for her to know the truth before she marries him than after. He'll be caught sooner or later. You can see that, can't you?'

Iris hesitated, then she nodded.

'Yes ... all right. I'll get a carbon for you. It shouldn't be difficult. I've some filing to do this afternoon. I'll have it for you tonight.'

But she didn't. Calvin had seen Travers meet her and had watched them drive away together. He had locked up the bank and had gone over to the restaurant and had sat at his usual corner table. He had ordered the lunch, and while waiting, his mind had been busy.

He was pretty sure Iris was telling Travers about the portable typewriter. What would Travers do? Get a search warrant? They couldn't open all the deed boxes. But they wouldn't need to find the Remington. All they would have to do would be to check the carbon copies of letters in the files. Once they did that, he was sunk.

The waitress put a plate of soup in front of him and mechanically he began to eat the soup.

Why get a search warrant? he thought, when Iris could take a carbon and give it to Travers to check! That was the obvious thing for her to do. Well, all right, he would watch her. But if she failed to get a carbon, what then?

He hurried through his meal and returned to the bank.

He went to the steel filing cabinets and locked them, removing the key. Then he went into his office and sat at his desk.

Iris returned to the bank at the same time as the auditors arrived. Calvin let them in. He glanced at Iris, noticing she looked tense. She moved past him and went into the washroom.

For several minutes, Calvin was busy with a customer. He saw Iris come out of the washroom, go to her desk, pick up the carbon copies of the letters she had typed and walk over to the filing cabinet.

Calvin cashed the cheque the customer had given him. He paused as he counted the money as he saw Iris try to open one of the files. He handed the money to the customer, nodded to him, then walked over to where Iris was standing.

He held out his hand.

'I do the filing here,' he said with his charming smile. 'I have my own system. Alice made such a mess of it. I had to reorganize the system. I'll still do it.'

Iris gave him the carbons without looking at him.

'There are some statements on your desk that want entering,' Calvin went on, taking the key of the file from his pocket and unlocking the cabinet. 'Will you go ahead and do them, please?'

She forced herself to meet the probing blue eyes. There was a jeering expression in them that made her feel sick. Ken was right! She was now sure this man standing before her was not only a thief but a murderer. In that brief moment as they stared at each other, she had an instinctive feeling that he knew she knew he had murdered Alice.

As she walked back to her desk she had to fight down a surge of panic that left her trembling.

2

Soon after four o'clock, James Easton left the sheriff's office and walked over to the bank. He had been receiving continuous and useless reports since dawn, his ulcer hurt him and he was tired and discouraged. So far, the Remington hadn't been found nor had anyone come forward with further information about Johnny Acres.

Every Remington typewriter but one in Pittsville had been checked from the list received from the local agent. The one still to be checked was the machine supplied five years ago to the bank.

Easton had no hopes that it would be the one he was hunting for. He only decided to check this machine himself as it would give him an opportunity to talk to Calvin.

Easton was a man easily impressed and Calvin impressed him. Calvin was just the kind of man that Easton would have liked to have been. Easton always wanted to play golf, but had never succeeded in getting out of the rabbit class. He envied tall, powerfully-built men. He envied men with Calvin's charm and ease of manner. He was satisfied Calvin had more brains than the sheriff, Travers and himself put together. If there was anyone who could find a clue to this Johnny Acres, Easton felt sure it would be Calvin.

He was at a dead end with the case and with the excuse of checking the bank typewriter, he hoped to get a lead from Calvin that might give him the chance of getting the bank reward . . . and how he wanted that money!

He walked up the path to the bank entrance and rattled on the letterbox. By now the bank was shut. There was a delay, then the bank door opened and Calvin looked inquiringly at him.

'Can you spare a moment, Mr. Calvin?' Easton asked, mopping his face with a grimy handkerchief. 'Or are you busy?'

'I'm busy, but come in,' Calvin said. 'We're doing an audit. Anything urgent?'

'Well ... not urgent. You've got a Remington typewriter here, haven't you?'

Calvin's friendly smile broadened.

'Come in ... do you want to buy one?'

As Easton moved into the bank, Calvin shut and locked the door.

'We're still hunting for this Remington ...' Easton began, but Calvin put his hand on his arm and steered him firmly towards his office, saying, 'You look fagged out. You've been working too hard. Come into the office and take the weight off your feet.'

Easton allowed himself to be propelled into the office, but not before he noticed Iris at her desk, staring at him. Easton never missed a pretty girl and he thought Iris was exceptionally pretty. This guy Calvin had all the luck. He was going to marry that sensational Kit Loring and now he had this girl to replace Alice. Easton thought of Mavis Hart. She wasn't a patch on this kid with her large eyes and her silky, wavy hair ... not a patch.

Calvin closed the office door, waved Easton to the armchair and went around the desk and sat down. 'Cigarette?'

Easton grimaced.

'Don't touch them ... I reckon they're sheer poison.'

'You're probably right ... I thrive on poison,' Calvin said and lit a cigarette. He moved his letter opener slightly to the right. Although his expression was friendly and frank, his mind was seething with sudden panic. Had Travers told Easton about the portable? He would have to be careful. Travers must know now the portable belonged to Kit. 'What's all this about a typewriter?'

'We've been checking the Remingtons sold to people here in Pittsville,' Easton said. 'I see five years ago, a Remington was delivered to the bank. We're looking for the machine this guy Acres used. Can I see the bank machine?'

'You certainly could if we still had it,' Calvin said and grinned. 'To my knowledge we haven't had it for the past year. I remember Alice telling me it was knocked off the counter and it was a complete write-off. Alice borrowed a machine for a time. She gave it back just after I came. I used mine which was pretty hopeless and that broke down: now I have borrowed my fiancée's . . . it's out there now: a Smith Corona portable.'

Easton shrugged his fat shoulders. He hadn't thought for a moment that the Remington listed at the bank would be the one he was looking for.

'I was just checking,' he said. 'Got to tick off every machine on the list. Now we'll have to start at Downside. That's going to be a hell of a job. There are over five hundred Remingtons in use there.'

Calvin drew in a lungful of smoke and relaxed. The past three minutes had made sweat run down his back.

'How's it going? Getting anywhere?' he asked.

'I guess not,' Easton said and scratched the side of his neck. 'We have this guy sewn up, but we can't get a lead on him. He did a smooth job. There were no fingerprints on the car. Records don't know him. We may catch him through the typewriter, but somehow I don't think we will. I think he was smart enough to cover his tracks even to the typewriter. He probably went to some typing bureau, typed the letter and paid a fee to use the machine. I know that's what I would have done in his place.'

And that's what I should have done, Calvin thought. I wish I had! That Remington could fix me even if this dimwit doesn't realize it.

'Well, I wish you luck,' he said. 'That reward is worth having . . . sixty thousand dollars! Phew! I bet Travers is sniffing around hoping to get his hands on it.'

Easton scowled. Calvin had read his thoughts correctly. All day, Easton had been thinking that Travers could beat him to the reward. The thought had been agony to him. Travers was smart. Somehow, he had to find this guy Acres before Travers did. That reward meant a fresh start for him: a new life.

'Have you any ideas, Mr. Calvin?' he asked, leaning back in his chair, folding his hands across the ache in his stomach. 'I mean . . . what would you do in my place?'

Calvin shrugged, smiling.

'I wouldn't know. I've no experience of this kind of thing. You're trained to the job.' He paused, then went on just as Easton was about to say something, 'But if I were in your place, I'd concentrate on all the out-of-the-way restaurants and cafes in the district to find out if anyone noticed Alice there. It seems to me when she sneaked out three or four times a week when she should have been working for her exam, she must have gone somewhere unless, of course, they just sat in the car and petted, but I don't think Alice was the petting type. I think Acres must have taken her somewhere: some roadhouse or restaurant. Alice never went anywhere and she would fall for that kind of thing where they have music and soft lights . . . you know the romantic angle. I think if you checked all the places within thirty miles or so of Pittsville you might find the place where he took her. It's a long shot, but I'd try it. You might find out, once you have found the place, where Acres was staying. Can't you get a photograph of Acres made up from the description you have of him and get it in all the papers and on TV?'

'We're doing that,' Easton said, his eyes suddenly alight, 'but that other idea of yours isn't so lousy. I'll work on it.' He got to his feet. 'Well, I mustn't keep you. That's a pretty girl you've found. Who's she?' He jerked his thumb to the door and winked.

'That's my future daughter-in-law,' Calvin said. 'She is going to marry Travers.'

Easton felt as if he had bitten into a quince. Everyone got himself a fine-looking dish except himself, he thought.

'Lucky guy,' he said. 'Well, be seeing you.'

They walked across the bank to the door.

Iris watched them. She had heard what Easton had said about the typewriter. She looked anxiously at him as he shook hands with Calvin, a genial smile on his fat face. She could see Calvin had fooled him.

A little after six o'clock, Calvin told her to go home. He leaned against the counter, looking at her, a sensual, jeering expression in his eyes.

'Well, I hope you enjoyed your first day here,' he said. 'I'm sure we're going to get along fine together. I won't be back before eight. These auditors will stick here until the last minute, but they are finishing tonight.'

Iris was glad to leave the bank. She walked quickly to the bus stop, and after a few minutes' wait, got on the bus that would drop her close to her home.

Leaving the bus at the road junction, she began the short walk to the rooming-house. She quickened her steps when she saw Ken's car drawn up on the grass verge and Ken, himself, leaning against the car, a smoking cigarette between his fingers.

'Hello there,' he said, coming towards her. 'I've just got back from Downside. I've got to be at the office by seven. I thought I'd wait for you. Any luck?'

Quickly she told him what had happened. He looked at her worried, distressed expression and he saw she was scared.

'He's smart,' he said and put his arm around her. 'Okay.

I'll have to think of something else. Anyway, this let's you out. You can leave it to me from now on.'

'No!' Iris pulled away from him. 'I feel the way you do now, Ken. This is something between us and him. He won't be back until eight o'clock. I'm going to look in his room. There's just a chance the money is there. If it isn't, I'll try the bank.'

Now it was Travers's turn to look worried.

'This guy's a killer,' he said. 'If he caught you at it . . . no, better not. You leave this to me.'

'I'm going to look in his room,' Iris said quietly. 'Tell me what to do.'

Travers hesitated, then knowing this was the one short cut to the reward, said, 'Well, make it fast. Three hundred thousand dollars in small bills takes up a lot of space. Look under the bed, in his drawers, in any suitcase. If you find a locked suitcase, see how heavy it is. Call me if you find anything, but be careful no one hears you make the call. One more thing, take a duster with you in case he comes back unexpectedly. You can say you were dusting his room as Flo hadn't time to get around to do it. Okay?'

A little pale, but determined, Iris nodded.

'Yes.' She kissed him. 'If I find anything, I'll call you.'

He looked at his watch.

'I've got to get going. The old man is waiting for his supper.' He put his arm around her and kissed her. 'Don't do it, honey, if it scares you.'

'I'm going to do it.'

She watched him get in his car and drive away, then she walked quickly towards the rooming-house. The upper floors were in darkness. As she opened the front door, she could hear the television blaring. She paused to listen. She heard sounds coming from the kitchen. She guessed Kit was preparing dinner. She hung up her coat, then went to the closet under the stairs and found a duster. As she began to mount the stairs, the kitchen door opened abruptly and Kit stood in the doorway.

Iris paused.

'So you're back. Seems funny to have you back at this hour,' Kit said, leaning against the doorway, looking up at Iris. 'Much more respectable than coming in at two in the morning. How do you like working with my handsome fiancé?'

'It's all right,' Iris said, aware blood was rising to her face.

Kit stared intently at her. Her face was white and sweat beads made a pattern on her upper lip. Iris could see she was very drunk.

'I'm so glad. Did he touch you? He has exciting hands.'

'Kit! Please!'

'Don't be so modest. You should know by now what men are like. If he ever touches you like that, tell me. I'll kill him. I've told him so. Just tell me.'

Iris turned and ran up the stairs. She paused at the head of the stairs to listen. She heard Kit's unsteady steps as she moved back into the kitchen and she shivered, then steeling herself, she went straight to Calvin's room.

She paused for a moment outside the door, then she turned the handle, eased the door open and entered the room. Crossing the room in the semi-darkness, she pulled the blinds, then she groped her way back to the light switch and snapped it on. She tucked the duster into the belt she was wearing and looked around the room.

There were very few places of concealment. First, she looked under the bed, but there was nothing there. Standing in a corner of the room was a suitcase, well worn and travel battered. She lifted it, but it was empty. She went to the big closet, opened it and saw at a glance it only contained shirts and underwear. She moved the various

157

articles aside, making sure there was nothing concealed under them. She opened the second drawer, working hurriedly, her heart beating with growing panic. The drawer contained handkerchiefs and ties.

Sure now the money couldn't be concealed in this room, she turned off the light and moved cautiously into the passage. She heard heavy footfalls coming up the stairs and her heart skipped a beat. She peered over the banister rail. Calvin was coming up the stairs, humming tunelessly, moving purposefully and quickly.

She hastily stepped into Kit's room and closed the door. She listened, hearing Calvin enter his room, hearing the light switch click down.

She leaned against the wall, her heart slamming against her ribs, her breath coming in stifled gasps. She waited there in the darkness.

Calvin had seen the light in his window as he had driven into the garage. He had got away earlier than he had expected. Leaving the car, he had gone to the front of the house and looked up at the lighted window. He wondered who was up there. At first, he thought it might be Kit, then it flashed through his mind it was more likely to be Iris.

He came quickly up the stairs and entered his room, surprised to find the light out. He turned it on. It must have been Iris, he thought. So she was spying for Travers! Well, all right: the time was rapidly approaching for a show-down with her. This was getting too uncomfortable and too dangerous.

Deliberately heavy footed, he crossed the room to the communicating door, turned the handle and walked into Kit's room.

Hearing him come, Iris snapped on the light. She faced him, realizing how white she had gone. Calvin regarded her with his confident smile.

'Why, hello! Was it you in my room just now?'

He watched her hesitate, then she said in an unsteady voice, 'Yes ... Flo had forgotten to dust ... I – I said I would do it.'

His smile widened.

'How very nice of you. I thought it was Kit up here.' He stepped back, his blue eyes jeering. 'Well, I'd better have a wash. I expect dinner is almost ready. I got back sooner than I expected.'

Iris didn't say anything. She wondered if he could hear the thumping of her heart.

Nodding, he closed the door. She stood listening to his tuneless humming as he moved around his room and she pressed her hands to her breasts.

CHAPTER FIVE

I

THE following day was Saturday. It was a relief for Iris to know she wouldn't have to spend the whole day in Calvin's company. They drove together to the bank. The auditors had finished their work and had gone back to San Francisco. While Calvin went through the mail, Iris did the routine jobs Calvin had shown her how to handle. Then Calvin dictated some half-dozen letters and Iris got busy with the typewriter while Calvin looked after the odd customer who came in.

Some minutes before eleven o'clock, when Iris brought the letters in for his signature, Calvin leaned back in his chair and stared expressionlessly at her.

'I have to go to 'Frisco this afternoon,' he lied. 'The old man wants to go over the audit with me. There's a train at twelve-thirty. The next one doesn't leave until three o'clock. If I don't catch the twelve-thirty train, I'll mess up my whole week-end. If I leave here at eleven-forty-five, I'll just catch it. Do you feel capable of locking up?'

Iris had trouble in controlling her excitement. Here was the opportunity she had been waiting for, and it had come so soon! With Calvin out of the way, she would be able to search the bank! If the money was there, she would find it!

'Why, yes, of course,' she said, controlling the eagerness in her voice.

Watching her, Calvin saw her reaction and could almost read what was going on in her mind. He had difficulty not to burst out laughing.

'I shouldn't be doing this,' he said. 'There's always a chance that someone will come in at the last moment, but they never have so far. I'll leave you a float just in case. You'd better have the keys to the vault.' His smile widened. 'You never know, I might have a pile-up or something.' He slid two keys across the desk. 'You have the key to the front entrance. Okay?'

'Yes.'

With a hand that was far from steady, Iris picked up the two keys.

He handed her a pile of papers.

'Would you enter this lot for me?' He looked at his watch. 'I'll have a wash.'

As soon as she had returned to her desk, Calvin left his office and went down the short passage towards the men's room. He paused in the passage and listened, then moving quickly to the back entrance to the bank, he silently unlocked the door and drew back the two heavy bolts.

Then he moved silently into the men's room and rinsed his hands. His tuneless humming was continuous.

Iris was so strung up, she could only stare at the papers lying on her desk, trying to think where she had best start her search when Calvin had gone.

She had plenty of time, she told herself. Better not do this on her own. As soon as Calvin had left she would telephone Ken and ask him to come over. Then together, they would search every likely hiding place in the bank.

She suddenly felt Calvin close to her and she reared away, nearly toppling off her stool. A thick, muscular arm went around her shoulders, steadying her. His touch made her flesh creep, but somehow she managed not to wrench away from him.

'Day dreaming,' he said lightly, releasing her and moving back. 'That's not the way to get the work finished. Well, I must get off. Sure you can manage?'

'Oh, yes.' Her voice was husky.

'Have a nice week-end. I'll be back Sunday night. Going somewhere with Ken?'

'I hope so . . . if he isn't tied up.'

'Of course . . . he is chasing the mysterious bank robber.' Calvin stared at her. 'You two will be sitting pretty if he collects the reward.'

Iris didn't say anything.

'What will you do with it when you get it?' Calvin asked. 'Sixty thousand . . . it is a lot of money.'

'We haven't got it yet,' Iris said unsteadily.

Calvin's smile was jeering and yet sympathetic.

'Sensible girl . . . I also never count my chickens. All the same, I wish you luck.'

He turned abruptly away and went back into his office. A few minutes later, he came out carrying a briefcase.

'Well, I'm off,' he said. 'See you Sunday night.' He lifted his hand in a half wave, then smiling at her, he walked out of the bank.

Iris waited a few moments, then slid off her stool and went to the window. She watched Calvin walk across the road to where his car was parked. She watched him get into the car and drive fast up the main street. She didn't move until she had lost sight of him, then breathing fast, her heart thumping, she went over to the telephone and dialled the sheriff's office. There was a delay, then Sheriff Thomson came on the line.

'This is Iris Loring,' Iris said. 'Can I speak to Ken, please?'

'Hello, Iris,' the sheriff said. 'Sorry, but Ken's with Easton at Downside. Anything I can do?'

Iris's heart sank.

'No, thanks. It's personal. Do you know when he will be back?'

'Can't say I do. Not until five o'clock, if then. Shall I tell him you called?'

'No, don't do that. It's nothing important. I was just wondering if he was working this afternoon.'

'He's working all right,' the sheriff said, his voice suddenly gloomy. 'So am I. We're trying to catch this bank robber. Come to that, how are you enjoying being a bank clerk?'

'I like it fine,' Iris said, trying to make her voice sound as if she meant what she was saying. 'Well, thanks.'

'You're welcome,' the sheriff said and hung up.

Iris replaced the receiver. She told herself she couldn't miss this opportunity. If Ken couldn't help her, then she would have to search the bank on her own. What a triumph for her, she thought, as well as for Ken, if she found the money!

She looked at her watch. It was now five minutes to twelve. She got off her stool and went to the bank door. The main street as usually happened on a Saturday morning was deserted. She stood by the door waiting for the church clock to strike the hour. It seemed a long wait. When finally, the mellow notes of the bell began to strike, she quickly shut the door and locked it.

With a sudden urgent feeling of panic, she went into Calvin's office and looked through the unlocked drawers of his desk. She found nothing to interest her. There was a steel filing cabinet against the wall. This was also unlocked and contained only papers relating to the bank's affairs. She paused to look around the room. There was no other place of concealment so she went down the passage into the men's washroom. A quick glance around the room told her here again there were no places of concealment.

If the money was anywhere, it had to be in the vault.

She took the keys Calvin had given her from her skirt pocket and went down the stairs to the vault door. She unlocked the two locks, pushed open the door and turned on the light.

She paused in the doorway, looking around at the deed boxes that were stacked along the three walls to the ceiling. The fourth wall was occupied by the safe. This she had no interest in as she had been with Calvin when he had opened the safe. It contained only the bank ledgers and cash taken at the end of the day.

She decided if the money was anywhere it would be in one of the deed boxes. She suddenly realized what a shrewd idea it would be to hide the money in one of these boxes. She put a stool against a pile of deed boxes and climbing on to the stool, she lifted down the top box. It was locked.

She tried the second box without moving it and found that too was locked. She remembered seeing a bunch of keys in Calvin's desk drawer. Maybe, she thought, there was a master key among the keys which would open all the boxes.

She went back to Calvin's office just as Calvin came silently into the bank, using the unlocked back door. He heard her in his office and he waited, breathing gently through his thick nostrils, his fleshy face hard and his blue eyes glittering. He heard her leave his office and he peered around the corner of the wall and watched her walk down into the vault. He closed the door, turned the lock and slid the bolts home. Then moving like a shadow, he entered his office, put his briefcase on the desk and took off his hat and coat. Unconsciously, he hummed softly under his breath. He stood by his desk, listening. He heard Iris moving the deed boxes, dumping them down on the floor, the clash of steel against steel coming clearly to him.

He rubbed his fleshy jaw with his thick fingers and his mouth set into a cruel, satisfied grin. This would be the showdown, he told himself. It was time. This girl was becoming a nuisance: not only a nuisance, she was dangerous.

He moved silently out of his office and headed for the vault.

In the vault, Iris had found the master key that opened the deed boxes. She had opened three of the boxes and was preparing to open the fourth. This was only full of documents and she continued with her task until she came to the last box of the stack. She turned the lock and lifted the lid and caught her breath sharply. In the box, neatly packeted, were packets of fifty-dollar bills. She had never seen so much money. As she stared at this money, she knew she had found the stolen payroll. She knelt, careless of her nylon stockings, staring down at the contents of the box, her heart beating wildly.

Calvin stood on the top step leading into the vault and watched her. All he could see of her was her rounded hips as she squatted, her narrow shoulders and her blonde hair. He moved silently down two more steps and shut the door to the vault. As the door closed, the catch of the lock made a sharp click . . . a sound in the silent vault that was as loud as the snap of a mouse-trap.

Iris jerked around. At the sight of Calvin, her body froze into motionless terror. They looked at each other. Calvin smiled his charming smile. Her terror excited him. Looking at her, he thought how much prettier, how much more desirable this girl was compared to Kit.

'Congratulations,' he said. 'Now, I suppose you'll begin planning how you will spend the reward?'

Iris could only stare at him. She could scarcely breathe. She knew it would be useless to scream, and she fought down the scream that rose in her throat. Down in the vault no cry for help could possibly be heard.

'For your information,' Calvin said, 'the famous

typewriter is in the deed box to your right and the famous fawn overcoat that I wore when playing the role of Johnny Acres is in the box next to it.'

He moved down two more steps and then paused.

Before she could stop herself, Iris jerked out, 'Don't touch me!'

Calvin's smile widened. He looked very handsome and sure of himself as he looked towards her.

'My dear girl, why on earth should I touch you?' he asked. 'You mustn't be frightened of me.'

Iris wasn't deceived by this chilling charm. She backed away until she pressed against the steel wall of the deed boxes.

'We'll have to talk about this, won't we?' Calvin said. He stooped to pull a deed box towards him, then he sat on it. 'You may think this is simple, but it isn't. Nothing is ever simple.' He took out a pack of cigarettes and shook a cigarette into his large hand. He lit the cigarette, squinting slightly through the smoke as he watched the girl's white, frightened face. 'Everyone is under the impression that Alice helped the mysterious Mr. Acres steal the payroll. She didn't.' He paused, then went on, 'Does Travers think I am Johnny Acres?'

Hypnotized by the quiet, deadly voice, Iris could only nod.

'I thought he had got on to me,' Calvin said. 'He's a bright boy . . . he'll go far . . . with luck. You, of course, are working with him? You both imagine you are going to collect the reward, send me to the gas chamber, then live happily ever after. That's the idea, isn't it?'

Iris didn't say anything. She had a horrible feeling she was very close to a violent death. The sight of this fleshy-faced man as he sat calmly staring at her, knowing he had murdered Alice, knowing she was now trapped in the vault with him turned her sick with terror.

'I don't think it is going to work out that way,' Calvin said. 'As a matter of fact, I knew what you were up to. I knew you wanted a carbon of one of the bank letters to give to Travers. I knew you were suspicious about the type-writer. That yarn I told you that I had to go to 'Frisco was so much blah. I wanted to catch you red-handed ... I have.'

Still Iris couldn't bring herself to say anything.

'Well, now we know the facts: you're spying for Travers and I am a bank robber, so let's get down to negotiations,' Calvin said, flicking ash from his cigarette. He glanced at his wrist watch. The time was twenty minutes past twelve. He wondered if Travers was expecting Iris. It would be awkward if Travers came over to see what was keeping her. There was still time, but he mustn't waste it. 'I think you can help me. I want to get this money out of Pittsville. You probably know the police are searching every car, checking all parcels and baggage that leaves here. It occurred to me that being the fiancée of the deputy sheriff, you could get the money out of Pittsville for me.'

Iris drew in a long, shuddering breath.

'You – you must be mad!' she gasped.

Calvin laughed.

'Oh, come, be intelligent. I'm not mad. I'm an oppor-tunist, and this is an opportunity. You are about the only person in this dreary town, apart from the police, who could take the money out safely. On Monday, I'll fix it for you to go to 'Frisco on bank business. You'll stay over-night. You will take with you a suitcase and in the suitcase will be the money. You will ask Travers to drive you to Downside Station. He'll do it. With him as an escort, you'll have no trouble getting the money out. You will leave the suitcase at the 'Frisco left-luggage office. You will give me the check. When I'm ready, I'll leave here and collect the money. It's not a bad idea, is it?'

Iris was so astonished, she forgot her fear.

'I wouldn't help you if it's the last thing I do! You must be mad to suggest such a thing!'

'My dear girl,' Calvin said patiently, 'you'll do it. You'll have to do it. Let me explain: the woman everyone thinks was Alice: the one in the car with me was your mother.'

Iris stiffened, staring at him.

'Is it so hard to believe?' Calvin asked. 'Your mother was the one who started all this. It was her idea that she and I should steal the payroll. It happened this way . . .'

Speaking slowly and deliberately, his eyes never leaving her white, frightened face, Calvin told her the whole story: how it was Kit's idea that they should steal the payroll and how, together, they had planned to shift the blame on to Alice. 'Once we had agreed to this idea,' Calvin went on, 'we had to decide what to do with Alice. It was Kit's idea we should murder her. I was against it at first, but she persuaded me . . . she is very persuasive when she isn't drunk. So between us, we killed her.'

Iris listened, petrified. At first, as his voice droned on, she refused to believe what he was saying, but as he went on and on, giving details, she suddenly realized that what he was saying was the truth.

'So you see,' Calvin concluded, dropping the butt of his cigarette on the floor and putting his foot on it. 'you'll have to co-operate. I don't suppose you'd be happy to be the cause of your mother going to the gas chamber, would you?'

Iris hid her face in her hands. She felt faint. The airlessness of the vault closed in on her. The horror of what she had listened to paralysed her.

'Your mother is very unreliable,' Calvin went on. 'If I had known she was an alcoholic I wouldn't have listened to her. When she's drinking heavily, I can't control her. All she thinks about is getting her hands on the money. It's driving her crazy knowing it is right here in the vault and she can't spend it. That's why I'm asking you to help me. If you don't take the money out of Pittsville, your mother is likely to do something that'll land not only me but her in trouble . . . and I mean trouble.'

'I won't listen to any of this!' Iris said wildly. 'I don't believe it! Kit would never do such a thing! Let me out of here!'

She made a sudden dash past him to the vault door. He turned on the deed box and caught her wrist, stopping her. She screamed and struck at him, her fist caught his temple. He grabbed her other wrist and pulled her to him. He was on his feet now, his breathing came through his thick nostrils in short, hard snorts that horrified her. He was grinning at her, his eyes blazing with a crazy fire that turned her cold. She ceased to struggle and stood against him, staring at him. He touched her; his hand moving over her body, making her shudder, then his hand dropped away. There was a long pause, then slowly and reluctantly, he released her and moved away.

'You're very attractive,' he said, 'but I'd better not . . . I want your help. You've got to help me. If you don't, your mother will go to the gas chamber. I promise you that.'

Iris backed away.

'I'll do nothing for you,' she said shakily.

'You will,' Calvin said. 'You'll either do what I say or your mother will die. Of course you will.'

He stepped to the vault door and pulled it open.

'Go ahead. I'm not stopping you. We'll talk again over the week-end.'

Iris went up the steps and into the bank. She snatched her coat from the hook and walked unsteadily to the bank door. She unlocked the door and went down the path into the deserted main street.

Very sure of himself, Calvin watched her go.

169

Travers got back from Downside a little after six o'clock. He found the sheriff still at his desk, pawing through a mass of papers that lay before him.

'Anything new?' the sheriff asked, leaning back in his chair and reaching for his pipe.

'I've been checking those Remingtons,' Travers said and dropped into a chair. 'Nothing so far. Easton's gone off on a wild goose chase checking the roadhouses around the district. He seems to think Acres must have taken Alice some place, and a roadhouse seems as good a bet as anything.'

The sheriff chewed his pipe.

'Suppose they did go to a roadhouse: where does that get us?'

Travers shrugged.

'He's clutching at straws. We've got to try everything I guess. I'm pretty certain Acres is still here. I'm pretty certain the money is here too. Sooner or later, he'll be tempted to make a false move, then we'll have him. That's police work.' He dropped the match into the ash bowl. 'Iris called you around mid-day,' the sheriff said. 'She wanted to know if you'd be free this afternoon.' He grinned sympathetically. 'I told her you were trying to earn an honest living.'

'That's a fact,' Travers said, but his mind was immediately alert. He had told Iris they wouldn't be able to spend the Saturday afternoon together so she couldn't have telephone for the reason the sheriff had given. This must mean she had discovered something. She would be home by now. He glanced at the telephone, but decided not to call her with the sheriff listening in. He pushed back his chair. 'Anything you want me to do?'

'Why not?' the sheriff said and waved to the mass of papers on his desk. 'All this wants going through ... reports from the highway patrols.' He took out his heavy gold watch. 'I guess I'll go home. You young fellows can stand the pace better than us old 'uns. If anything turn up, call me. Those pesky thrip are at my roses again.'

When he had gone, Travers reached for the telephone. He called the rooming-house. Miss Pearson came on the line. When Travers asked for Iris, Miss Pearson said she wasn't in. She was the only one at home.

'She'll be back soon,' she said. 'I'll tell her you called.'

Travers thanked her and hung up. He wondered where Iris had got to, then shrugging, he settled down to work. It wasn't until he turned on the desk light that he realized the time was now half past seven and he had had no word from Iris. He called the rooming-house again. This time it was Kit who answered.

'Iris has gone to bed,' she said curtly. 'She had a headache.'

'She's not ill?' Travers asked sharply.

'She has a headache,' Kit said and hung up.

Kit had been to a movie at Downside. During the day, she had been depressed and had a premonition that something bad was going to happen. As soon as she had supervised the lunch for the old couple, she had changed and had driven to Downside where an Alfred Hitchcock film was showing. She felt she had to escape from the house. Although the film was up to Hitchcock's usual standard, it failed to hold her and she had to force herself to sit in the darkness, knowing that if she returned home, the feeling of depression would be there to haunt her. Finally, when the film finished, she went into the gathering dusk and crossed to a bar near where she had parked her car. She drank two double whiskies. Her tension slightly relieved, she got in the car and drove home.

She arrived back just after half past six. When she had put the car in the garage, she went into the kitchen to see that Flo had the supper in hand, then satisfied, she went up to her room.

She found Calvin sprawled in an armchair, the ashtray on the table by his side crammed with butts. He stared at her, his blue eyes glittering.

'Where the hell have you been?' he snarled. 'I've been waiting and waiting . . . where have you been?'

She closed the door and walked over to the dressing-table. Sitting down, she began to tidy her hair.

'When I want you in my room, I'll invite you,' she said, not looking at him. 'Get out!'

'Where's Iris?'

She paused, comb in hand and turned to stare at him.

'I haven't seen her. Why?'

Calvin rubbed his hand over his face.

'She knows.'

The comb slipped out of Kit's hand. It clattered on the polished boards.

'Knows? Knows what?'

'She knows you and I killed Alice.'

'You killed her! I didn't!' Kit said, her voice going shrill. She jumped to her feet. 'How does she know?'

Calvin lit another cigarette. His hands were unsteady.

'I caught her in the vault. She had found the payroll. I had to stop her mouth . . . either that or I'd have had to kill her. I told her you and I had pulled the robbery and you are as guilty as I am. That was the only way to stop her running to her boy-friend.'

Kit got slowly to her feet. She walked to the window and

stood looking out at the distant hills, her arms tightly folded across her breasts.

Calvin watched her, feeling uneasy. You never knew with an alcoholic. She might blow her top, he thought.

'It's all right,' he went on, his voice soothing. 'She's not going to give us away. I've talked her into seeing sense.'

'Get out of here!' Kit said in a low violent voice. 'Get out or I'll kill you!'

'Now don't start that nonsense,' Calvin said irritably. 'You and I are in this mess together. We've ...' He stopped short as she suddenly spun around and made a quick dash to the chest of drawers. He was startled how quickly she moved, but already tense, he was on his feet in a flash and had crossed the room as she wrenched open the drawer. As her hand dipped into the drawer, he caught hold of her wrist. He had a glimpse of the gun as he jerked her away. She struck at him. He caught her flying fist and flung her from him. As he scooped up the gun, she threw herself at him, panting, her eyes glittering, her face chalk-white. Again he shoved her off. She was helpless against his great strength and she went sprawling on the floor. Taking the gun, he backed to the door.

'Cut it out!' he snarled.

She lifted herself up on her arm, her white face was ugly with hate.

'Give me that gun!' she said, but she didn't attempt to get to her feet.

'Shut up!' Calvin said furiously. 'Having you around is enough to drive anyone nuts.' He slid the gun into his hip-pocket. 'Get up and stop looking at me like that! Go on ... get up!'

She got slowly to her feet and crossed to a chair and sat down. She ran her fingers through her hair in a desperate, despairing gesture.

'Has Iris been in at all?' Calvin demanded. 'She left the bank at half past twelve. Did she come home?'

Kit shook her head.

'Wait here,' Calvin said, and went down the stairs to Iris's room. He knocked on the door. Getting no answer, he turned the handle and looked into the room which was empty. He went to the closet and opened it. A quick look inside, a quick look in the drawers of the chest told him she hadn't taken her clothes. Where was she?

Had she decided to tell Travers? She hadn't been home now for six hours. What was she doing?

He went back to Kit's room. Kit was still sitting motionless, her head buried in her hands.

'I don't know where she is,' Calvin said, 'but if Travers telephones tell him she has a headache and has gone to bed. I've got to talk to her before she sees him unless she's seeing him now.'

Kit didn't look up. After staring at her for a few seconds, Calvin shrugged and went to his room. He closed the door, then taking the gun from his hip-pocket he was about to put it in a drawer of the chest when he had second thoughts.

He was very uneasy. Had Iris decided to give him away? He thought it was unlikely, but she was young and the decision might have been too much for her. Well, if she had told Travers and if they tried to arrest him, they would have a job on their hands. He wouldn't be taken alive. He wasn't going to spend weeks in jail and then be taken like an animal to be slaughtered. He put the gun back in his hip-pocket. If Travers started something, he'd land up with a bellyfull of lead.

He washed his face and hands. The time was now close on seven-fifteen. He forced himself to sit down. He lit a cigarette and tried to relax, but he was too tense. He immediately got to his feet and began to prowl around the room.

He heard Kit go downstairs. He waited a moment, then went out and leaned over the banister rail. He heard Kit talking to Flo. He rested his thick arms on the banister rail and listened.

Suddenly he heard the telephone bell ring. The sound sent a wave of hot blood up his spine. There was a delay, then he heard Kit say, 'Iris has gone to bed. She has a headache.' There was a pause, then she said, 'She has a headache,' and he heard the receiver drop back on its cradle.

He drew in a long, slow breath of relief. That would be Travers. At least Iris hadn't contacted him. But where was she?

As he looked down the two flights of stairs into the hall, he suddenly saw Iris. She came in silently, took off her coat and hung it on the hall rack, then slowly she began to mount the stairs.

Calvin drew back. He listened. When he heard her enter her room, he moved quickly and quietly down the stairs and paused outside her door. He could hear Flo saying good night. He heard the click of the back door as Flo left. He still waited. He heard Kit begin to put the finishing touches to the dinner, then he gently turned the door handle and entered Iris's room.

Iris was standing, her back to him, looking out of the window. She glanced over her shoulder as he came in and she stiffened. She turned swiftly to face him.

'What do you want?' she demanded, her voice shaky. He could see she had been crying. Her face was white and drawn. 'I don't want you in here!'

He closed the door and leaned against it.

'Have you made up your mind what you are going to

do?' he asked. 'Kit knows. I told her. Our lives are in your hands. Are you going to help us?'

'I don't know,' Iris said. 'I must talk to Kit. Please go away.'

Calvin studied her, then he nodded.

'Yes ... you talk to her, but remember this: she's as guilty as I am. Give me away and you give her away. Just remember that.'

He went out of the room and back to his own room.

At eight o'clock, the dinner bell sounded, and Calvin went downstairs. The meal was set on hot plates on the sideboard. Neither Iris nor Kit made an appearance. Calvin served the old couple, chatting to them, telling them that Iris had a headache, probably due to the change in her work, and all the time he talked, he listened for sounds that would tell him what was happening upstairs, but he heard nothing.

In her room Kit took from the closet a bottle of whisky and poured herself a stiff drink. She drank the whisky, then poured another drink. She lit a cigarette and then moved to the armchair and sat down, still holding the bottle of whisky. As she began to relax and as she was deciding to have another drink, the door opened and Iris came in.

CHAPTER SIX

I

IT was Sunday after lunch. Kit, Iris and Calvin sat in the lounge. Miss Pearson and Major Hardy had gone to their rooms for a nap. Kit and Iris were both pale and silent. Calvin was relaxed and very confident.

'It's one of those things,' he was saying to Iris. 'You can't go through life without some of the gilt being rubbed off. I admit it: we shouldn't have done this thing, but we did it, and now we have to make the best of it. Three hundred thousand dollars is a lot of money. If you think about it, you'll realize why we were tempted. I'm sorry about Alice. She just happened to get in the way, so . . .'

'Shut up, you swine!' Kit screamed at him.

Iris closed her eyes and her hands turned into fists. For the past twelve hours she had been through a nightmare. The sound of the violent, drunken voice of the woman who was her mother sickened her.

Calvin's eyes blazed with fury. He half started out of his chair, then controlled himself.

'If you scream like that,' he said, an edge to his voice, 'the old people upstairs will hear you.'

Kit stared at him, her face convulsed with hate.

'Then stop talking . . . do something!'

'There's nothing I can do. If anyone is to do anything it will have to be Iris.' Calvin twisted around in his chair to look directly at Iris. 'If you want to save your mother from the gas chamber, you'll have to help. You'll have to see Travers and tell him you had the chance to search the bank yesterday and you found nothing. You'll tell him you went through all the deed boxes and found nothing relating to the robbery. You'll give him a carbon of one of the bank letters. I have one ready for you. I went into Downside yesterday and typed a letter on a Remington in a typing bureau. You've got to convince him he has made a mistake in picking on me. Do you understand?'

Kit was watching Iris anxiously. Iris continued to stare down at her hands. She didn't say anything.

'After you have talked to Travers,' Calvin went on, 'you'll go to 'Frisco on Monday and you'll take the money with you. Once it is out of Pittsville, your mother will be safe. If it is found here, she won't be safe. Don't imagine I'll let them arrest me without dragging her into it. Once I have the money in a safe deposit in 'Frisco, your mother and I will leave here. You'll be free to marry Travers. You can then forget about us. I expect you'll be glad to.'

Still Iris said nothing.

'Well, come on,' Calvin said, his voice suddenly impatient. 'What are you going to do? You can't just sit there like a dummy. Are you going to help your mother or aren't you?'

Iris looked up and stared at Kit, then she said quietly, 'Yes.' She got to her feet. 'I'll do what you want. When I go to 'Frisco, I'm not coming back. I hope I'll never see either of you ever again.'

She went out of the room. Calvin got quickly to his feet and followed her. She was putting on her coat. He gave her the carbon copy of the letter. She took it without looking at him, then turning away, she opened the front door and walked quickly towards the garage.

Calvin watched her drive to the highway, then shrugging

his heavy shoulders, he returned to the lounge. Kit had lit a cigarette. She stared at him as he came in.

'Well, that's that,' he said. 'She'll do it. In less than a month you'll have your share of the money. I told you it would work out, didn't I?'

'Get out of my sight!' Kit said softly. 'And keep away from me! I don't want the money. You take it. I'm not touching it. I want you out of here. Do you understand? Pack up and get out! I won't have you in this house. You're evil. Get out!'

'It's not going to be that easy,' Calvin said. 'We have got to stay together. I've explained why and I'm not going over it again. For the next year or so, you and I are going to be Siamese twins. Don't think I like it. I don't, but there is no other way. And don't talk about not taking your share. You'll take it once you see it. Don't kid me you won't.'

He went out of the room. Kit suddenly covered her face in her hands and began to cry.

Travers had Sunday duty. He had just finished a sandwich lunch when he saw Iris drive up and park her car outside the office. He hastily tossed the paper bag into the trash basket and wiped the desk free of crumbs, then he got to his feet and went to the door just as Iris entered.

'Hello, honey. I was getting worried about you,' he said, kissing her. Immediately he was aware something was wrong. He drew back to look at her. She was pale, and there were dark smudges under her eyes. She looked steadily at him. 'What's up? he asked. 'Come in and sit down.'

Iris sat with her back to the light.

'It's nothing,' she said. 'I had a headache.' She forced herself to smile. 'I'm all right. Ken ... we were wrong. It isn't Calvin. I'm sure of that now.'

Travers went around and sat behind his desk.

'What's new then?' he asked sharply.

'He went to Downside yesterday and left me the keys,'

Iris said, speaking rapidly and looking down at her hands. 'I went through the whole bank. I even opened all the deed boxes. The money isn't there nor the Remington. Look, I have a carbon copy of the letter you wanted.' With hands that shook a little, she opened her bag and gave him the carbon. She watched him study it, then he grimaced. 'The Remington we're after didn't write this,' he said and laid the carbon down. Something was wrong, he told himself. Why did she look so ill? Why, when she told him she had found nothing in the bank, had she avoided looking at him? 'Well, that seems to be that,' he said. 'I was practically certain Calvin was our man. He still could be. He might have hidden the money somewhere else. I'm not giving him up as a suspect. We haven't anyone else.'

'You've got to give him up as a suspect!' Iris said. There was a note of hysteria in her voice. 'My mother is marrying him! You can't hound him now!'

'But look, honey,' Travers said uneasily, 'the fact you didn't find the money and this carbon doesn't match the Remington doesn't prove Calvin didn't do the job. I still think he did. I think he's smart enough to fool us, and I'm not staying fooled.'

Iris got to her feet.

'I can't stop you,' she said, 'but I don't have to be on your side any longer.' She pulled off her engagement ring and placed it on the desk. 'I'm going away, Ken. You must please yourself what you do. I don't want to marry you. I've thought about it. I don't want to marry someone working for the police.'

Travers stared at the ring as if he couldn't believe his eyes. Then as Iris made for the door he jumped to his feet and came quickly around his desk.

'Iris! Wait! You can't do this! Let's talk about it. You just can't break our engagement like this.'

She paused.

'I'm sorry, Ken, but I have to go away. I don't know where I'm going yet. Tomorrow I'm going to 'Frisco for the bank. When I get there, I'll decide what I'm going to do. I have to get away from here. I've decided I'm too young to get married. I want to look around. I'm sorry.'

Travers went red and then white.

'So that's it? It's suddenly occurred to you, I'm not good enough. So you want to look around. Well, for Pete's sake! Have you gone crazy or something?'

'I just want to look around,' Iris said. 'I'm sorry, Ken. I think it would be better if you forget about me. I hope you will,' and she went out and over to her car.

Travers made a move to go after her, then stopped. He went around the desk and sat down. He stared for some minutes at the modest emerald and diamond ring, then he reached out, picked it up and put it in his pocket.

He sat brooding for some minutes, then getting to his feet, he locked up the office, got in the sheriff's car and drove fast to the rooming-house.

He rang the bell and waited. There was a long pause, then the door opened and Calvin looked inquiringly at him.

'Hello,' Calvin said. 'Are you looking for Iris? She's out.'

'I wanted to see Mrs. Loring,' Travers said, staring at the big man.

'I'm sorry: Kit's resting.'

'I still want to see her,' Travers said in his cop voice. 'Will you tell her I'm here?'

Calvin's smile became a trifle forced.

'Is this official business?' he asked. 'I don't want to disturb her.'

'Call it that if you like,' Travers returned. 'I want to see her.'

Calvin stood aside.

'Come in. I'll tell her.'

Travers walked past Calvin into the lounge. He watched Calvin go upstairs. Travers moved around the room impatiently. There was a long delay, then Calvin came down the stairs.

'She's coming. She's powdering her nose.' He moved into the lounge and made to sit down.

'This is a personal thing,' Travers said curtly, 'I want to see Mrs. Loring alone.'

Calvin raised his eyebrows.

'Of course. I wasn't thinking.' He moved to the door. 'Kit isn't in very good form. Be careful how you handle her.' Nodding, he went out of the room.

Travers continued to wait. After some minutes, he heard slow hesitant steps coming down the stairs, then Kit appeared in the doorway. He could see at once that she had been drinking. She had also been crying. Her face was white and puffy. Her eyes glittered. She faced him.

'Well? What is it?' she demanded, her voice loud and harsh.

'It's about Iris,' Travers said. 'Something's upset her pretty badly. Can you tell me what it is?'

'If I knew, I wouldn't tell you,' Kit said, peering at him as if she had trouble in focusing. 'I don't want you here. If you want to know what's upset her . . . ask her.'

'Did you know she is going away?' Travers asked patiently. 'She's broken off our engagement. I want to know why. I think you can tell me.'

Kit's lips twisted into a sneer.

'Why shouldn't she go away? What's her future if she stays in this one-horse hole? I'm glad she's going. I'm glad she has had the sense to break off with you. She's young enough and pretty enough to hook a rich husband: not a small-time cop like you!'

'Okay,' Travers said evenly. He had to make an effort to

control his temper. 'You must have talked her into this. Well, I now know where I stand. For her sake, I hope she does hook a rich husband if that's what she wants.'

Kit stared at him, her brown eyes hating him, then she turned and moved unsteadily out of the room. Just as she reached the doorway, she lurched and had to steady herself by grabbing hold of the door.

Travers watched her. She moved on into the hall and as she started up the stairs, she again lurched. Travers felt a sudden cold rush of blood up his spine. Into his mind flashed a picture of Alice Craig, wearing that awful coat and the floppy hat concealing her face as she had come out of the bank on the night of the robbery. She too had lurched in exactly the same way as this woman had lurched. Then he had thought she had been ill, but now in a sudden intuitive flash he realized that he hadn't been watching Alice Craig. The woman he thought was Alice, had been Kit, wearing Alice's clothes. It had been Kit who had come out of the bank that night and that meant it was Kit who had helped Calvin steal the payroll! It had been Kit who had helped Calvin murder Alice!

Travers felt suddenly sick. Kit! Iris's mother!

Watching him through the crack in the door, Calvin saw by Travers's expression, he had guessed at the truth. He drew back. A few moments later, Travers came out and walked to the front door. Calvin watched him go.

His sweat-moist hand rested on the butt of the gun in his hip pocket. He wondered what Travers would do.

2

It was after eight-thirty when Travers who had been sitting in his car at the bottom of the road for the past half hour, saw Iris coming towards him in Kit's car.

He jumped out and stood in the middle of the road, waving. Iris pulled up. Travers came up to her.

'We've got to talk,' he said. 'I'll leave my car here. Let's go up to Perch Lane. We can talk there.'

'I don't think I want to talk to you,' Iris said, not looking at him. 'I'm sorry, Ken. Talking will get us nowhere now.'

'Oh yes, it will,' Travers said and walking around to the off-side door, he got in beside her. 'Let's go.'

Iris hesitated, then made a U-turn and drove back to the highway. Neither of them said anything until they had reached the top of Perch Lane, a favourite meeting-place of theirs. It was dark now. The lights of Pittsville twinkled at them from a distance as they sat side by side.

Travers said abruptly, 'I know now why you are leaving. I know why you've broken the engagement. I want you to know I'd have done exactly the same thing if I had been in your place.'

Iris stiffened with shock. She looked quickly at him: fear in her eyes, then she looked away.

'I know your mother is involved in the robbery,' Travers said quietly.

Iris shuddered. Suddenly, she began to cry. Travers put his arm around her. He held her to him as she sobbed, her body trembling, her hands gripping his. It was some moments before she managed to control herself, then she moved away from him, dabbing her eyes with her handkerchief.

'What are you going to do, Ken?' she asked unsteadily. 'I'm going out of my mind. It's too horrible to think of. When that awful man told me ... oh, Ken! Kit of all people!'

'There is only one thing to do,' Travers said. 'I've been thinking about this. We've got to consider ourselves first. You and I are going to leave town. We're going to get married. Your mother won't object ... she can't object now. I'm resigning from the police. There's no other way out. Your mother and Calvin will have to work out their own destiny, but I'm not having anything to do with it.'

Iris looked searchingly at him.

'But what will you do? You can't leave the police. It's your job.'

'I'll find something else. I'm not worrying about that now. I can't remain on the force knowing what I know. We've got to clear out or else we could be in serious trouble.'

'He – he wants me to take the money to San Francisco tomorrow,' Iris said. 'He says if I don't ... Kit ...' She choked back a sob. 'I said I'd do it.'

'You're not doing it. That's what I mean when I said we've got to clear out tonight otherwise you could get involved. Once you are involved, you'll be an accessory to murder. So don't let's argue about it. We're leaving tonight.'

'But where do we go?' Iris asked. 'I haven't any money ... We just can't go.'

'I have some money,' Travers said. 'It isn't much but it's enough to keep us going for three or four months. We'll take the eleven fifteen train to 'Frisco. In the morning, we'll get married, then I'll start looking around for something to do.'

Iris hesitated, then she nodded, gripping Travers's hand.

'All right. I'll come with you. Whatever you say, I'm sure you're right.'

'Fine.' Travers took the engagement ring from his pocket. He offered it to her. 'Do you want your ring back, Mrs. Travers?'

At half past nine, Sheriff Thomson was about to settle down to watch a Western on TV when the front door bell rang. He looked at his wife, grimaced, then hauled himself out of his armchair and went to the door.

'Why, hello, Ken,' he said when he saw who it was. 'Don't tell me we've got an emergency on?'

'It's all right, Sheriff,' Travers said, following the sheriff into the small sitting-room. 'It's not that kind of an emergency.' He put his deputy's badge and his ·45 revolver on the table. 'I'm resigning from office as from this minute. I'm sorry to spring this on you, but there are special circumstances. Iris and I are leaving tonight for 'Frisco. We're getting married tomorrow. I'm quitting because I don't want to be a police officer when I marry her.'

The sheriff stared at Travers, then he walked heavy-footed to an armchair and sat down.

'Well! Do you have to drop this kind of bombshell in an old man's lap as late as this? What's wrong with being a police officer? Why can't you marry her and still remain a police officer?'

'Special circumstances,' Travers said woodenly.

'They must be. Don't you think I'm entitled to know what the circumstances are?'

'Yes, I do, but I'm sorry, Sheriff . . . I can't tell you.'

The sheriff pulled at his moustache.

'Look, son, you and I have worked together now for more than five years. I've known you since you were a kid. Let's have the truth. What's gone wrong?'

'I can't tell you,' Travers said. 'I've got to quit and that's all there is to it.'

'You'll be sheriff next year. You can't throw up your career this way, Ken. Have you thought of that?'

'Of course I have,' Travers said a little impatiently. 'I know what I am doing. I've got to quit, and I'm quitting.'

The sheriff shrugged.

'Well, okay, I guess I can't stop you.' He waved to the

badge and the gun. 'They're still yours. You can't walk out of the force in five minutes. It'll take a couple of weeks before you are officially free of us, but that doesn't mean I'll stop you quitting tonight if it's that urgent. All the same, hang on to the gun and your badge until your papers come through.'

'I don't want them,' Travers said. 'As far as I'm concerned, I'm officially off the force as from now.'

The sheriff got to his feet.

'Sure you don't want to tell me? You can trust me, Ken. I think you could do with some help.'

Travers smiled tightly. He held out his hand.

'Thanks, Sheriff, but there's nothing I want to say.'

The two men shook hands.

'I guess this damn bank robber is going to get away with it,' the sheriff said gloomily. 'I was counting on you to get him. This job is way out of my class and out of Easton's class too.'

'If he's to be caught, he'll get caught,' Travers said woodenly. 'I'll get in touch with you. So long for now and thanks for everything.'

He went out to the waiting car. Iris looked questioningly at him as he got in beside her.

'That's number one problem out of the way. He took it all right. Now we'll go to your home for you to pack a bag. I'll wait outside. If there's trouble, you call and I'll fix it.'

'There won't be any trouble,' Iris said.

Ten minutes later, they pulled up outside the rooming-house.

'Go ahead and pack what you want,' Travers said. 'We should be moving in about an hour. If you want me, I'm right here.'

As Iris entered the hall, she heard music from the TV filling the house. She went quickly up the stairs to her room. Shutting the door, she found a couple of suitcases and hastily began to pack them. This took a little time, but finally she finished. As she was trying to shut the lid of one of the cases, Calvin said, 'Can I help?'

She spun around, her heart missing a beat. He was standing in the doorway, watching her, a fixed, ugly grin on his face.

She backed away as he moved into the room and shut the door.

'Go away!' she said, terrified. 'Don't come near me!'

'What's all the excitement about?' he asked mildly. 'What's all the packing for? You're not leaving, are you?'

'I'm leaving with Ken tonight,' Iris said, trying to steady her voice. 'He's outside . . . waiting for me. Now get out!'

'You have a little job to do for your mother tomorrow. You can't leave until then.'

'I'm not doing it! Ken knows . . . get out!'

Calvin moved to the window and looked down at the waiting car in the drive. A hot, scalding rage ran through him.

'What is he planning . . . to jail your mother?' he asked, turning and staring at her.

'He's resigning from the police. We're getting married. Please, go away!'

'You mean he isn't going to do anything about Kit nor – me?'

'That's what I mean.'

Calvin thought for a long moment, then he switched on his charm.

'Why, that's wonderful. Maybe it's better for you two to be out of the way.' He crossed the room and shut the lid of the suitcase with a squeeze from his powerful fingers. 'I'll carry your bags down.'

Iris didn't say anything. She watched him pick up the

two bags and walk out of the room. For a moment she stood motionless, trying to control the trembling of her body, then she went quickly out of the room and up to Kit's room. She turned the door handle, but the door was locked.

'Kit . . . it's me. I want to talk to you.'

There was silence.

She knocked.

'Kit . . . please . . . I'm going away: please open up.'

A loud, drunken voice exclaimed. 'Oh, go to hell for all I care! Go away and keep away!'

Iris stepped back, hesitated, then turned and went quickly down the stairs. Calvin was standing in the hall.

'Well, so long,' he said. 'Have a nice honeymoon. I won't embarrass the groom by coming out. You may not think it, but we'll get away with this. There's no opposition now. The boy who had me worried was your smart future husband.'

Iris picked up the two bags and without looking at him, went out to where Travers was impatiently waiting.

Calvin watched them drive away, then he walked upstairs and into his room. He sat down and lit a cigarette, he was much more confident now. Of course it was tiresome that Iris wasn't taking the money out, but at least, he now only had an ageing sheriff and that fool Easton to worry about. There must be some way to get the money out. The great thing was he was rid of Travers.

Around eleven o'clock, he was still sitting, chain-smoking when the communicating door jerked open and Kit came in.

Calvin looked up.

Now for another scene, he thought irritably. She's been howling her eyes out and she's tight again.

'Where's Iris gone?' Kit asked, standing in the doorway.

189

'While you have been swimming in alcohol,' Calvin said, stretching out his massive legs, 'our problems have solved themselves. Iris very sensibly has decided to marry her cop who very sensibly, in view of the circumstances, has decided to resign from the police force. They have gone off together, and I imagine this will be the last time we see them. This is excellent for us because we now have a dotty old sheriff and a F.B.I. agent with stomach ulcers trying to solve the famous bank robbery. The chances of either of them solving it are remote, so for the moment we are sitting pretty.'

'She's marrying that boy?' Kit said, coming into the room.

'Why shouldn't she? He's smart. If I had a daughter, I'd be glad to see her marry our hero.'

'I owe you something, don't I?' Kit said, sitting down and staring at him with hate. 'How I wish I had never set eyes on you! You've spoilt my life. All I hope now is you'll suffer the way you've made me suffer.'

Calvin stifled a yawn.

'There's a chance, but I hope not, but life's damn odd. It catches up with you. Well, could you get over the dramatics? We have business to discuss. I have an idea.'

'I don't want to listen to any of your ideas!'

'You'll have to,' Calvin said. 'I told you: from now on we're going to be Siamese twins whether you like it or not. Tomorrow I'm resigning from the bank. At the end of the week we'll get married and who do you suppose is going to be our best man?' He grinned at her. 'This is where I'm playing it smart. Our best man is going to be our old pal, Easton. He's not only going to give us away, but he's going to put us on the train to Florida. How's that for a bright idea? We'll have him escort us to the train and he won't stand any nonsense about searching our bags. That guy likes me. I can talk him into anything.' Calvin's grin widened. 'Like it? It's a winner. In ten days, baby, we'll be out of here on our way to a spending spree.'

'Suppose I don't want to do it?' she said in a low, hesitant voice.

'You haven't any choice. It's either my way or you'll land up before a judge. Come on, snap out of it! We're going to get away with this . . . can't you see? We're nearly in the clear.'

'But we'll have to live with ourselves.'

Calvin leaned back in his chair. He drew in a slow, deep breath of exasperation.

'Just what does that mean?'

'You wouldn't understand,' Kit said. 'I'm only just beginning to understand. We should never have done this thing.'

'That's a very bright remark. We did it, now we have to take it as it comes. Look, you're drunk. You leave all this to me. All I ask you to do is to stay sober enough to go through the motions. I'll fix everything. You do as I tell you. Okay?'

As she didn't say anything, Calvin went on, 'We'll get a quick sale of this house. I'll put it in the hands of the agents tomorrow. Better break the news to the old dears. I'll write to my pal in Florida. I'll get him to send me a letter offering me a job. That'll square the bank. We'll have to get everything fixed as fast as we can. There's always the chance the top boy will take Easton off the job and put someone on as smart as Travers.'

Kit got slowly to her feet and walked unsteadily to the door. She paused and stared at Calvin for a long moment. There was an expression in her eyes that sent a sudden feeling of fear and uneasiness through him.

She turned and still saying nothing, she entered her room and closed the door between them.

CHAPTER SEVEN

I

CALVIN arrived at the bank early the following morning. He brought with him his hold-all and he parked his car close to the back entrance of the bank. He went immediately to the vault and packed the payroll into the hold-all.

The sight of the money restored his confidence. He went out the back way and locked the hold-all in the boot of his car.

That was the first step. He was sure he would be safe in moving the money now from the bank to the rooming-house. It was when he attempted to take the money out of Pittsville he would have to watch out.

He waited until nine o'clock, then he put a telephone call through to Marthy at head office. He explained that his replacement for Alice had suddenly gone off to get married and he needed another assistant in a hurry. Marthy promised to send someone as a temporary help on the next train. Then Calvin told him he had been offered a very good job in Florida. He intended getting married and had decided to give up banking. He said he would be glad if Marthy could release him at the end of the week.

Marthy immediately made difficulties. He pointed out that Calvin was under contract to the end of the month. The payroll robbery had still to be solved. Joe Lamb was still ill. It would be difficult to replace Calvin.

Calvin listened to all this with growing impatience.

'Just the same,' he said when Marthy had concluded, 'I'm quitting. I'll be out of here by the end of the week, and I'll be glad to be shot of this one-eyed bank and this one-horse town. If you think you can stop me, go ahead and try.'

'In that case,' Marthy said curtly, 'you will leave to-morrow. I'll send someone down right away to relieve you,' and he hung up.

Calvin dropped the receiver back on the cradle. He lit a cigarette and stared uneasily at the glowing tip. He had now burnt his bridge. He was out of a job. Maybe he shouldn't have talked that way to Marthy. Then he thought of the three hundred thousand dollars now locked in the boot of the car and he grinned. What was he worry-ing about? Who wanted to be a bank manager with all that money to spend? He called Easton's office.

A girl's voice answered. There was a slight delay, then Easton came on the line.

Calvin saw a customer come in. The man waited im-patiently to be served. Let him wait, Calvin thought, and asked Easton how he was. He listened to Easton griping about his stomach pains, then he cut in to tell him he was leaving the bank, getting married and going to Florida. He asked Easton if he would be his best man. Easton seemed to hesitate and Calvin wondered if he had rushed this too fast.

'This is pretty sudden, isn't it?' Easton said. 'What's the idea – going to Florida?'

'A pal of mine runs a restaurant there,' Calvin said. 'He wants a partner. It's an opportunity too good to miss. Kit will come in handy too. Look, I've got someone waiting for me. We get married on Saturday. Can I count on you?'

'Why, sure. Why not? Glad to help out.' Easton didn't sound glad. He was thinking enviously some people had all the luck. Here was this guy not only marrying a dish like the Loring woman, but getting himself a partnership as well. Talk about luck!

'Fine and thanks,' Calvin said. 'See you before then,' and he hung up.

He went out and cashed the customer's cheque. From then on, he was kept busy. It was nearly eleven o'clock when the telephone bell rang. Calvin had two customers to serve and he let the bell ring. He became irritated when the bell continued to ring. Finally, when the customers had gone, he went into his office and snatched up the receiver.

'This is Sheriff Thomson,' the sheriff said. 'I was beginning to think I wasn't going to get an answer.'

'I'm single-handed,' Calvin snapped. 'What is it?'

'Could you get down to Bentley's store right away, Mr. Calvin?' the sheriff asked. 'You know where it is? The big store they're building on Eisenhower Avenue. When I say right away, I mean right away.'

Calvin thought the sheriff had gone off his head.

'What do you mean?' he snarled. 'I don't close the bank for another hour yet. What do I want with the store?'

There was a pause, then the sheriff said, 'I'm sorry, Mr. Calvin, I'm trying to break this gently. There's trouble down there . . . Mrs. Loring . . .'

Calvin felt as if an iron mailed fist had slammed against his heart. He clutched hold of the telephone receiver so tightly his finger nails turned white.

'Mrs. Loring?' His voice turned husky. 'What . . . what . . .?' He made an effort and pulled himself together. He went on, his voice under control, 'Let's have it, Sheriff. What's the trouble?'

'She's up there on the scaffolding . . . the part where they're building. She's threatening to jump.'

Cold sweat fell on Calvin's hand. Threatening to jump!

If this rumdum killed herself there was the letter to be opened by her attorney: *in the event of my death.*

'What are you doing about it?' he found himself yelling.

'Take it easy. We're doing all we can, but there isn't much we can do. The fire brigade is standing by. We've got men talking to her, but she won't listen. I thought maybe you could talk her into some sense.'

'Yeah ... how long has this been going on? How long has she been up there?'

'About half an hour. Can you get down here right away, Mr. Calvin?'

'I'm coming,' Calvin said and slammed down the receiver. He walked quickly out of his office.

There was a man waiting at the counter: a fat, peevish-looking character who drummed on the counter with well-manicured finger nails.

'How much longer do I have to wait?' he demanded. 'I want to cash a cheque.'

'The bank's shut!' Calvin said violently. 'Clear out!'

The man gaped at him. His fat face fell to pieces at the sight of Calvin's expression.

'Go on ... get out!' Calvin snarled.

The man backed away, turned and hurried out of the bank. Calvin shut the doors and locked them. Then he ran out the back way where his car was parked.

He was thinking: this is it! You were crazy to have hooked up with an alcoholic. Unless I do something, she'll kill herself, and then I'm finished. I shouldn't have let her out of my sight! Well, I asked for it and now I've got it!

He climbed into his car and drove the half-mile fast. As he swung into Eisenhower Avenue, he saw the crowd and his heart kicked against his side.

A policeman waved him to a halt.

'I've got to get through,' Calvin said, leaning out of the

car window. 'Sheriff Thomson wants me to talk to the woman. She's my fiancée. Get me through, will you?'

The policeman stared at him, recognized him and then nodded.

'Okay, sir. You keep going slowly. They'll let you through.'

He stood back and blew his whistle, motioning to another policeman some way ahead.

As Calvin edged his way through the crowd, he saw firemen standing by an escape and looking up. He saw men, women and children, with horror on their faces, also looking up. He controlled the impulse to stop the car and look up himself. He edged the car to the second policeman who shoved his way through the crowd towards him, his red face aggressive. 'What the hell do you think you're doing? Where do you think you're going?' he demanded.

'She's my fiancée,' Calvin said in a hard, curt voice. 'They think I can talk her down.'

The cop's aggression went away.

'Leave the car,' he said. 'You won't get through this lot in a car. Sheriff Thomson is waiting for you.'

Calvin got out of the car. At the back of his mind, he remembered there was three hundred thousand dollars locked in the car's boot. Out of the car, he looked up, following the gaze of some hundreds of people.

There was a new wing being added to Bentley's store. The new wing consisted only of scaffolding and steel piping. Out on this skeleton foundation, some two hundred feet above the street was Kit. She was wedged in between the apex of a triangle formed by some of the steel poles. Her feet, one in front of the other, rested on one slim pole. A false move would send her down a long drop to death.

Calvin became rooted as he stared up at the distant figure. Kit was wearing slacks and a leather windcheater.

She was smoking and seemed completely indifferent to the people staring up at her.

'There you are,' a voice said and a hand gripped Calvin's arm. With an effort he dragged his eyes from the perilously perched figure and stared blankly at Sheriff Thomson. 'She's in a bad way,' the sheriff went on. 'We've been up there, but when we get within fifty feet of her, she threatens to jump. Think you can do anything?'

Aware now everyone was staring at him, Calvin said, 'I don't know. I'll try. She's drunk, of course.'

The sheriff pulled at his moustache.

'How she managed to get out there without falling beats me. Working from where she is, the boys get taken up in a crane bucket. She just walked out there as if it was the sidewalk.'

'Can you get me up in the bucket?' Calvin asked.

'Sure. Maybe if she sees you, she'll let you get her in, but watch it – she's jumpy.'

They forced their way through the crowd until they reached the crane bucket. They paused by the bucket to look up. Kit flicked her cigarette butt into the air. They watched the tiny white end come spiralling down to the ground. It seemed to take a long time before the crowd parted slightly to let it fall on the sidewalk. A souvenir hunter pounced on it.

'You okay for heights?' the sheriff asked looking at Calvin's white face. 'Better not go up there if you're not. It's a long way up.'

Calvin climbed into the bucket.

'I'm all right,' he said. 'Just get me up there.'

'Don't look down and don't lean your weight on the sides . . . it could tip. Good luck,' and the sheriff signalled to the crane driver who was perched even higher than Kit in his small, glassed cabin.

As the bucket moved slowly upwards, the crowd gave a

great sigh of excitement. They looked from Calvin, standing in the bucket and then to Kit who was watching him as he was lifted towards her.

The crane driver took him up gradually. Finally, Calvin swung exactly opposite Kit. They were within twenty feet of each other.

Because of the steel scaffolding, it wasn't possible for the crane driver to get Calvin closer. Calvin, gripping the edge of the iron bucket, was sickeningly aware of the awful drop below.

'Hello,' Kit said. 'I've been waiting for you. I knew you would come.'

'Well, here I am,' Calvin said, forcing his voice into steadiness. 'What the hell's got into you? Can you get over here? I'll see you down.'

Kit laughed.

'Come and fetch me. You've only to get out of that ridiculous thing and walk along that rod and then duck under this one and you're with me. Come on: you and I could take the quick way down.'

Calvin wiped his face with the back of his hand.

'What's got into you? What's the idea – pulling a stunt like this?' He scarcely knew what he was saying. 'It's not going to get you anywhere. Come on. Cut this out! I'll help you if you'll come.'

'When I'm ready,' Kit said, 'I'm jumping, but I'm not ready yet. You've made me suffer, now I'm going to make you suffer. I'm staying here until I'm good and ready, then it's going to be the quick way down. When I hit the ground, you'll have about twelve hours – not more – of freedom. It'll take my attorney about that long to remember the letter I left with him. When he opens it, you'll be on the run. That'll be the moment, when you begin feeling as I've felt these past weeks.'

Calvin stared at the white, drawn face.

'I have the money,' he said. 'Three hundred thousand dollars. It's in the boot of my car. We can still get away with this, Kit. Easton has promised to be our best man. He'll get us out of Pittsville. Tell you what I'll do: I'll give you three-quarters of the money if you'll chuck this and come down. How's that?'

Kit opened her bag and took out a pack of cigarettes. With a nonchalant disregard of her position, she lit a cigarette and then flicked the spent match down to the staring crowd.

'Didn't you hear what I said?' Calvin said, raising his voice. 'Think . . . by the end of the month, we'll be out of this – you and I, with money to spend. Come on: what's the sense of getting so far and then doing a thing like this?'

She blew a long wisp of smoke at him.

'I've told you . . . but you don't seem to understand. I have to live with myself, and I find I can't do it. I didn't think it would be like this.' Her pale lips parted in a cynical smile. 'I have Alice on my mind: day and night. I see the poor thing in my dreams. I can't get her out of my mind. So . . . I'm taking the way out that you'll have to take before long.'

'Okay, if you're that gutless,' Calvin snarled. 'Go ahead, but why involve me? That letter of yours . . . do something about it. Look, I'll . . .'

Kit's jeering laugh cut across his frenzied voice.

'That's the trick in this,' she said. 'You thought you had it all fixed, but you're not getting away with it . . . as I'm not getting away with it. When I go . . . you'll follow. You shouldn't have involved Iris in this. That's something I'll never forgive you for. We'll settle this thing together . . . I'll go first, but make no mistake about it, you'll go second.'

Then for no reason that Calvin could see, her foot slipped and she dropped her bag as she snatched at the nearest steel pole. She missed and fell. Calvin involuntarily shut his eyes, feeling a cold wave of blood surge through him. He heard a loud moan come up from the crowd: a woman screamed. He forced himself to look.

Kit had fallen no more than ten feet. She had caught hold of a scaffolding pole and was now hanging in mid-air.

Calvin was now above her, looking down at her. He watched her swing herself from an impossible position into a safe position with the carelessness of a monkey swinging from tree branch to tree branch. In the moment that had chilled his blood, she was once again settling herself into the precarious safety of yet another apex of yet another triangle of steel.

The crane driver, watching all this with morbid fascination, expertly lowered the bucket so Calvin was again on the same level and facing Kit.

'Did you think I was going to die?' she asked. He could see she was completely unshaken. 'Heights mean nothing to me. When I'm good and ready, I'll let go, but I'm not ready yet.'

From her expression Calvin knew it was hopeless to try to persuade her into any sense. For a long moment, he tried to force himself to get out of the bucket and climb over the perilous rods to her, but he hadn't the nerve. He was sure that if he did reach her, she would take him with her in a fatal drop to death.

'For the last time, Kit,' he said, 'cut this out. We've everything to gain. Can't you see . . . we can get away with it . . . it's in the bag!'

'Give me a cigarette,' she said. 'I've lost mine. I must have a cigarette.'

With a shaking hand, he took from his pocket his pack of cigarettes and carefully tossed the pack to her. His spine tingled when she let go of the steel rod to catch the flying pack. For a moment, she wobbled uncertainly, then she recovered her balance.

He pleaded: 'Kit! Come on down. We can work this thing out together . . .'

She suddenly screamed at him in a voice that reached the crowd below, 'Get the hell away from me! You can't talk me into anything. Get away or I'll jump!'

The sudden change of her expression, the glare in her eyes warned him he could do nothing with her. He waved to the crane driver, pointing down.

The crowd below gave a satisfied, sadistic sigh as Calvin was slowly lowered to the ground. The show was to go on.

2

Four hours later, Kit was still up there and the crowd, still fascinated, remained in the congested street.

During these four long hours a police officer, a doctor and finally a priest had gone up in the crane bucket, one after the other, to try to persuade her to come down. All of them had failed. She had remained there, indifferent to what they said, smoking cigarette after cigarette and looking down at the sea of up-turned faces without any show of emotional stress.

Calvin sat on the stone edge of the town's fountain. From this vantage point, he could see Kit clearly. With him was the sheriff and a doctor from the hospital.

'If she stays up there until it is dark,' the sheriff said, 'we plan to rig a net under her. Then some of the boys will go after her. It'll be tricky. I guess I'll put a searchlight on her to blind her. She mustn't see the boys fixing the net.'

'I don't think she'll jump now,' the doctor said in professional, pompous tones. 'The longer she stays up there, the less likely she is to take the plunge. I agree about the net, but we'll have to wait until it's dark.' He glanced at his watch. 'Another five hours.'

Listening to them talk, Calvin thought: You two dopes don't know Kit. She'll jump, damn her! When she's ready, she'll jump and she won't give you a chance to rig a net. This is her idea to make me suffer! I wish I knew if she had really written that letter! If she hasn't I haven't a care in the world, but if she has . . . I'm wasting time just sitting here. With all this fuss going on, I might be able to get out of town. I'd have a twenty-four-hour start on them. But could I get out? The road blocks are still in place. Without Easton to okay me, they're certain to check the car, and then I'd be sunk.

He felt a sudden, over-powering urge to do something. The past four hours had strained his nerves to breaking point. He just couldn't continue to sit there for another five hours before it was dark enough for them to try this cock-eyed scheme of rigging a net.

He got to his feet. His fleshy face was congested, his eyes were wild.

'I'm going up again,' he said. 'I can't just sit here. This is driving me crazy.'

'I don't think it will serve any useful purpose,' the doctor said. 'I'd leave her alone, Mr. Calvin. When it's dark . . .'

'You're not me!' Calvin snarled. 'That's my future wife up there! I'm going to talk to her again.'

The doctor shrugged his shoulders.

'Be careful. Standing like that in the hot sun for so long must have imposed a . . .'

'Oh, stuff it!' Calvin said and shouldering his way through the crowd he reached the bucket. The crane driver was still at his post, and as soon as he saw Calvin waving to him, he started the crane engine.

'Hey! Calvin!'

Calvin turned. Easton, his fat face white, sweat streaming into his collar, came through the crowd and joined him.

'I heard it on the radio,' Easton spluttered. 'I couldn't believe it. I hopped in the car and here I am.' He stared up. 'Jeepers! What's got into her?'

Calvin's mind was busy. This was the man he needed to help him get out of Pittsville. He caught hold of Easton's arm.

'I'm glad you came,' he said. 'She's gone crazy. She's been up there four hours now. I'm going up there to see if I can persuade her to come down this time. I've already been up, but maybe this time, she'll come down.'

'Anything I can do?' Easton asked, his eyes still rooted with horror at the figure perched far above him.

'Maybe there is ... will you stand by?' Calvin said. 'This is cracking me. I'm relying on you. Don't go away.'

'Like hell I won't,' Easton said, delighted that a guy like Calvin should want him. 'You take it easy. I'm right with you.'

Calvin got into the bucket and waved to the crane driver. He was hoisted into the air. After what seemed an interminable time he was level with Kit. The sight of her alarmed him. The strain of standing for so long in that perilous position was telling on her. Her face was chalk white and drawn, but there was a hard glitter in her eyes that warned him she had still plenty of resistance left.

'Hello,' she said. 'Are you enjoying yourself?'

'Are you coming down?' Calvin asked, a snarl in his voice. 'Haven't you had enough?'

'Have you?'

'Sure: I've had more than enough. Cut this out and come down!'

He saw her hesitate, then she said, 'I don't think I can. I've got cramp. I could use a drink!' She stared at him. 'If I come, will you help me?'

'I'm not getting out on to those rods,' Calvin said. 'I wouldn't trust you not to try to take me with you. I'm not helping you. You got yourself into this jam . . . get yourself out of it!'

'I can't. I'll come if you'll help me. I'm so stiff I can scarcely move. If you'll help me, I'll marry you and go away with you. I can't get down without your help.'

Calvin stared suspiciously at her.

'This is a sudden change of mind, isn't it? I thought you intended to jump.'

'I've been up here long enough to change my mind. If you'll reach out, I can catch hold of your hand.'

'Oh no. You're not touching me. I'd rather trust a snake than you. I'll get the police up here. They'll get you down. I'm not helping you.'

The sudden blaze of hatred that lit up her eyes shocked him. He realized his instinct for danger had saved him. She had intended taking him with her.

'Come here, you devil!' she screamed. 'Let me get my hands on you!'

'Go to hell!' Calvin snarled and waved to the crane driver to lower the bucket.

Even as the bucket began to sink, Kit left the safe apex of the steel rods and sprang forward, her face ghastly with frustrated fury. In horror, Calvin saw her questing hands miss the rim of the bucket by inches. Had she caught the edge of the bucket, she would have tipped him out. She gave a long wailing scream and was gone.

Shuddering, Calvin shut his eyes. The roar of the crowd came up to him, then the sound of a sickening thud as Kit's body hit the sidewalk. The bucket swung down quickly.

Easton was waiting as Calvin climbed unsteadily out of

the bucket, his face ashen. The fat Federal agent caught hold of Calvin's arm, steadying him.

Fifty yards or so away, the crowd surged forward, their backs to Calvin. Two men in white coats tried to force their way through the crowd.

'Get me out of here!' Calvin gasped. 'I'm going to pass out! Get me out of here!'

'Okay, boy,' Easton said, his own face whitish-green. 'You hang on to me.'

Together, they fought their way through the crowd. No one paid them any attention. The crowd was only interested in seeing Kit.

'My car's right here,' Calvin said. 'Will you drive? Take me to the rooming-house.'

'Sure,' Easton said. 'I'm sorry. What made her do it? I can't say how sorry I am . . .'

Calvin slumped in the passenger's seat and hid his face in his hands. He had quickly shaken off the shock of seeing Kit fall, now he wanted time to think what the next move should be.

This is it, he said to himself. If the bitch has left a letter, I've only got a few hours before they'll come after me. I've got to get moving. The money's in the boot. Easton's driving. It's a perfect set-up, but will he do what I tell him?

He sat back with a groan.

'She was drunk,' he said, his hand sliding to his hip pocket. His fingers closed around the cold butt of the gun. 'I guess it was too much for her . . . she promised to give up drinking. But why she did that . . .'

'I didn't know.' Easton shook his head. 'Yeah, when they get drinking . . . can do anything.'

Calvin eased the gun out of his hip pocket and laid it on the seat between Easton and himself, keeping his large hand on it, hiding it from Easton. He stared thoughtfully at

Easton's profile: the fat weak chin, the indecisive mouth. He decided he could take a chance.

'Look, I've changed my mind,' he said, 'I want to get out of Pittsville. Drive me to Merlin Bay, will you? I feel I could do with the sight of the sea.'

Easton slowed to stare at Calvin.

'Why, that's the best part of a hundred and fifty miles, boy,' he said. 'I can't take you there. I've got work to do. Look, I'll take you . . .'

'You'll take me to Merlin Bay,' Calvin said, a grating note in his voice. 'Unless you want a slug of lead in your fat belly.'

He lifted the gun and dug it into Easton's side. The car swerved and recovered. Easton started to pull up, but the gun dug deeper into his side.

'Keep going . . . hear me?' Calvin said. The tone of his voice sent a chill through Easton. He hurriedly increased the speed of the car. They were on the highway now. The time was just after five o'clock: too early for the rush hour home. Only one or two cars passed them.

'Have you gone crazy?' Easton gasped. 'For Pete's sake! What do you think you're doing?' He had already taken a quick look and satisfied himself Calvin was holding a gun.

'Relax and do what I tell you,' Calvin said. 'Hasn't it got through your thick skull that I grabbed the payroll and killed Alice Craig?'

'Why . . . why . . .' Easton was so shocked he lost his voice.

'Kit Loring was in it too,' Calvin went on. 'That's why she jumped, the stupid bitch. She's left a confession with her attorney and that's why I've got to skip. Make no mistake about this, Easton, you make a wrong move and you'll get it . . . what have I to lose?'

Easton said in a quavering voice, 'You won't get far.

You'd much better give up. There's a road block a mile ahead. Give me the gun and I'll try to get the rap . . .'

'Shut up!' Calvin snarled. 'You're getting me through that road block! I have the payroll in the car boot and I'm going to get it through the road block if I have to kill you. You're going to use your rank as a Federal agent to get me through. If you don't, you'll be the first to get it!' Calvin dug the gun into Easton's fat side. 'Step on it. I'm not warning you again. If you can't stop them searching this car, you'll get lead in your fat gut. It'll take you days to die. Hear me? Days!'

His fat face like wax, Easton increased the speed of the car. In a few minutes, both men saw the road block ahead and three policemen waiting.

CHAPTER EIGHT

I

As the two interns slid the blanket-covered stretcher into the ambulance, Ken Travers came through the crowd. He stopped short at the sight of the stretcher, then seeing the sheriff standing nearby, pulling at his moustache, Travers went over to him.

'Is she dead?'

'Hello, Ken, where did you spring from?' the sheriff said, surprised. 'I thought you were in 'Frisco.'

'I heard it on the radio. I came straight back. Is she dead?'

'Yeah. She jumped while Calvin was trying to talk her down. Where's Iris?'

'I left her at the hotel. I guessed she would jump. I didn't want Iris here.'

'You're right . . . a terrible thing,' the sheriff shook his head. He moved back as the ambulance began to edge through the crowd. 'What got into her I can't imagine.'

Travers asked, 'Where's Calvin?'

The sheriff looked vaguely around.

'I guess he's somewhere. Poor fellow! They had planned to marry this Saturday . . . then this happens.'

Travers drew in a deep breath. Now Kit was dead, he was free to arrest Calvin. He could still earn the reward.

'Sheriff . . . you've got Calvin wrong,' he said. 'He is the man we're hunting for ... Johnny Acres. I've enough proof to arrest him.'

The sheriff gaped at him.

'Hey, son! What are you saying?'

'Lend me your gun, Sheriff. I'm not off the force yet. I want Calvin.'

The sheriff hesitated, then seeing the expression on Travers's face, he hauled out his .45 and handed it over.

'Sure you know what you're doing?'

'I'm sure. Where is he?'

The sheriff waved to a police sergeant who came over.

'Seen Mr. Calvin around?'

'He went off with Mr. Easton,' the sergeant said. 'They left together about ten minutes ago.'

'In Easton's car?' Travers asked.

'No ... in Mr. Calvin's, but Mr. Easton was driving. Mr. Calvin looked pretty bad. I guess Mr. Easton was taking him home.'

'Do you want to come, Sheriff?' Travers asked. 'I'll talk while you drive.'

Looking dazed, the sheriff got into his car and Travers got in beside him.

'We'll go to Mrs. Loring's place,' Travers said, 'and step on it. Calvin could run for it.'

'He has Easton with him,' the sheriff pointed out, sending the car shooting towards the highway.

'He's dangerous. If Easton isn't on to him ...'

'What is all this?' the sheriff asked, bewildered. 'What makes you think Calvin is our man?'

Travers told him.

Easton slowed the car as they approached the road block.

'Watch it!' Calvin said, his voice vicious. 'You get me

through and you'll be okay, but start something and it'll be the last thing you do start.'

Easton pulled up as one of the policemen moved towards him. Recognizing him, the policeman tossed him a casual salute. He turned and waved to the other two officers who lifted aside the wooden pole barring the road.

'Get going!' Calvin said. 'Step on it! Don't give them a chance to talk to you!'

Aware of the gun grinding into his side, his face white, sweat running into his eyes, Easton shoved his foot down hard on the gas pedal and the car surged forward. The policeman had to jump aside or Easton would have hit him. Calvin waved to the policeman as the car swept forward and stormed past the road block and out on to the open road.

I'm through! Calvin thought with a feeling of wild triumph. He looked back. The policemen were staring after them, but they made no move to come after the speeding car.

Easton was thinking: now what's going to happen? He must be out of his mind if he thinks he'll get away with this. But what's going to happen to me? He's already killed the girl. Why shouldn't he kill me?

Calvin removed the gun from Easton's side.

'Keep going,' he said. 'I didn't think it was going to be that easy.' He again looked back over his shoulder. There was no sign of any cop on a motorcycle. He relaxed, and shoving the gun under his thigh, he took out a pack of cigarettes. 'About a couple of miles further ahead, there is a side road to Bellmore. Take that.'

Easton flinched. He knew that road. It twisted up a hill for a mile or so, then went through a thick forest. During the week-ends it was crowded with picnickers, but for the rest of the week it was deserted.

He'll kill me there, he thought. That's what he aims to do.

'We'll stop there,' Calvin said as if reading his thoughts, 'and you can get out and walk back. That'll give me an hour's start. That's all I'll need.'

Easton knew he was lying. Although he had a gun in a shoulder holster, he knew he wasn't quick enough to get it out and kill Calvin before Calvin killed him. He had never been any good at drawing a gun. Up to now, he had taken care never to get himself in a position where he need draw a gun.

Calvin watched him. He saw the agony of fear on the fat face.

He knows I'm going to kill him, he thought. He's certain to be carrying a gun. I'll have to give it to him as soon as he stops the car. I can't risk letting him get out.

'Here we are,' he said as the side road came into sight. He lifted the gun and poked Easton with it.

Easton spun the wheel and shot the car along the narrow dusty road. Again Calvin looked back, but there was no one to see them turn off the highway.

That's luck, he thought, if they do come after me, they'll think I've gone to Merlin Bay. Once I get rid of this punk, I'll head for that air-taxi field at Bellmore. Once I get to 'Frisco, I'll lose myself.

Easton saw the forest ahead of him.

I've got to take a chance, he thought. He won't shoot until I've stopped the car. My only chance is to wreck the car. I'll be braced by the wheel. With any luck he'll crack his head on the windshield.

'Take it easy,' Calvin said. 'We'll stop at the top of the hill.'

With his heart hammering, Easton peered into the driving mirror.

'We've got company,' he said hoarsely.

Calvin jerked around to look through the rear window. Easton, panting, swung the wheel and drove off the road straight towards a fir tree. They were travelling at over fifty miles an hour. Instinctively, Easton braked a split second before the car hit.

Feeling the car swerve, Calvin turned his head. His finger tightened automatically on the trigger of the gun as he glimpsed the car about to crash. The gun went off as the car smashed into the tree.

Calvin felt a jolting shock. He was faintly aware of a rendering sound of crushing steel, then he blacked out.

2

Travers said, 'Well, that's it, Sheriff. That's why I resigned. I couldn't send Iris's mother to the gas chamber and that's what it would have meant. But now she's dead . . . it's different. I can go after Calvin.'

The sheriff drove in silence for some moments. His mind, still slightly stunned by what Travers had told him, slowly considered what to do. Finally, he said, 'Yeah . . . well, this is between you and me, Ken, but if it got out, you could be in trouble. I'd do my best for you, but you've stuck your neck out for an accessory rap.'

'Don't I know it,' Travers said. 'I'll have to take a chance on it. Hey! Stop! This guy may have seen them.'

There was a patrol officer on a motorcycle coming towards them. As the sheriff pulled up and waved, the officer swung his machine alongside the car.

'We're looking for a white Mercury,' Travers said. 'Mr. Easton was driving. Has it passed you?'

'Yeah,' the officer said. 'Passed me about ten minutes ago on the Merlin Bay road.'

'Merlin Bay?'

'That's it.'

'Thanks.'

As the sheriff engaged gear, Travers said, 'There's a road block three miles ahead. He's probably using Easton to get him through. That means he's trying to get out with the payroll.'

The sheriff grunted and shoved the gas pedal to the boards.

Four minutes later, they pulled up at the road block. The two officers said the Mercury had gone through ten minutes ago.

'Went through like a bat out of hell,' one of them said, scowling. 'Mr. Easton looked like he was ill. As soon as the pole was up, he charged through without saying a word to us. What gives?'

'Could be trouble,' the sheriff said. 'Let us through, Jack. We're in a hurry.'

Shrugging, the patrol officer signalled to his buddy to pull up the pole.

Travers said, 'Let me drive, will you, Sheriff? I know this car better than you do.'

'What you're trying to say,' the sheriff said, his voice frosty, 'is you think you can drive faster than I can. Well, son, I don't agree.'

With that, he trod on the gas pedal and sent the car roaring down the highway until it built up a speed of a shuddering eighty miles an hour.

'Take it easy!' Travers bawled above the roar of the engine, 'you'll break the poor old girl's back!'

The sheriff grinned stiffly and kept up the speed. They had gone some miles when Travers suddenly shouted, 'Slow up! Look at that!'

The sheriff braked.

'Look at what?' he asked, staring ahead.

'To your right. Look at that dust settling. A car's been up there recently. It's the short cut to the Bellmore airfield,' Travers said. 'It's my bet they've turned off there.'

The sheriff pulled up and leaned out of the window. He surveyed the faint cloud of dust that was slowly settling on the dirt road and he nodded.

'Could be you're right. Shall we try it?'

'Yeah, but take it slow.'

Five minutes later they reached the forest: a minute later they saw the wreck of the Mercury. The sheriff pulled up.

'Don't rush it,' Travers said sharply. 'Look, you stay here. I'll check. This guy's dangerous.'

'What do you mean ... I stay here! I'm the sheriff, aren't I? Give me my gun!'

'I'm handling this. I want the reward,' Travers said and forced a grin. He pulled out the sheriff's gun from his trouser's band and got out. 'Anything happen to me, you get the boys up here.'

He walked slowly towards the wrecked car. As he got closer he could see the lid of the boot was open. Then he saw a huddled figure sprawled over the steering wheel. He moved closer, his gun raised. He looked to right and then to left, then signalled to the sheriff.

The sheriff, muttering to himself, got out of the car and joined him.

'Easton ... dead,' Travers said.

Not fifty yards from them, Calvin lay hidden in a thicket. By his side was the suitcase containing the payroll. He was bleeding from a long gash down his face. His right leg was broken. His left arm was dislocated. He was only semi-conscious. How he had got himself out of the wreck, got around to the boot, forced it open, taken the suitcase containing the payroll and then dragged himself into the thicket he would never know.

He watched the two men carry Easton's lifeless body from the car and lay it on the ground. He watched Travers kneel beside the body while the sheriff stood by him, tugging at his moustache.

He looked from the two men to the sheriff's car that stood some twenty yards from the thicket in which he was hiding. Could he drive it if he could grab it? he asked himself. It was his only hope of escape. It should be possible even with his broken leg. He had only to use the gas pedal. He could steer with one hand. But where to go? The airfield was out. He couldn't arrive there in his condition. Maybe he could find some place . . . a farm . . . somewhere to hole up until the leg healed. With all his money, he should be able to buy his freedom.

It would mean shooting both the sheriff and Travers, but that didn't worry him. There was no other way out if he was to get away.

Travers, squatting on his heels beside Easton's body, suddenly stiffened. His keen eyes had seen that to the right of him the coarse grass was flattened. From the angle he was looking, he could see a path had been made through the grass as if something heavy had been dragged across it. He could see the path led directly to a thicket of shrubs.

Without looking at the sheriff, he said, 'Calvin's right with us. I think he's hiding in that thicket to your left. Don't look. He may be armed.'

'Easton got a gun?' the sheriff asked.

'He should have.'

Travers moved his body slightly so it screened Easton from the thicket. He opened Easton's coat, found the ·45 still in its holster and pulled it out. The sheriff squatted beside him. Travers slid the gun to him. Both men felt naked squatting here with their backs to the thicket.

'Don't rush it,' the sheriff said. 'We'll get around the other side of the car. You go right. I'll go left.'

They stood up.

Calvin raised his gun. His hand was very unsteady. He saw the two men rise and separate: each moving around the Mercury. He was suddenly sure they knew where he was. The sheriff was nearest to him and he quickly shifted his aim from Travers to the sheriff and squeezed the trigger.

The gun went off with a choked bang. The sheriff lurched forward and flattened face down on the grass. Travers jumped around the Mercury and knelt.

Calvin cursed. He couldn't see Travers now. Well, at least it was one against one, but Travers could move where he liked and Calvin couldn't.

Travers waited, restraining the impulse to go to the sheriff. He knew he would be a dead duck the moment he showed himself.

Very softly, he heard the sheriff say, 'I'm okay. A close miss, but he didn't get me.'

Travers drew in a long, deep breath.

'Stay where you are and don't move,' he said in a forced whisper. 'I'll try to get him from the rear.'

He began to crawl backwards, keeping the wrecked Mercury between himself and the thicket.

Calvin had a sudden premonition he wasn't going to get out of this trap. He thought of Kit.

You were a fool to have hooked up with her, he told himself, but maybe she was right. I should have stayed poor.

He looked at the suitcase lying by his side. Three hundred thousand dollars! He would never spend even a dollar of that fortune now . . . not even a dollar!

He thought of Alice. Maybe she was better off dead. He felt no remorse for her death. What would her life have been anyway? he asked himself.

He heard a faint crack of a breaking stick somewhere behind him. He turned his head. He saw Travers about twenty yards from him, coming out of the forest, moving slowly and cautiously, gun in hand.

Calvin snarled. He tried to turn but the pain in his leg made him feel faint.

Travers could walk right up to him and kill him like a mad dog. He couldn't get his gun around to bear on Travers.

Why wait?

Kit had taken the quick way out. She said he would follow her.

As Travers moved slowly forward, there was a sudden bang of a gun. He saw Calvin's massive body rear up and then flop back. A wisp of gun-smoke curled out of the thicket.

He paused, then seeing the sheriff get to his feet, he walked quickly towards the thicket.

>>> If you've enjoyed this book and would like to discover more great vintage crime and thriller titles, as well as the most exciting crime and thriller authors writing today, visit: >>>

The Murder Room
Where Criminal Minds Meet

themurderroom.com